The Android

Even the book morphs!
Flip the pages
and check it out!

Look for other [ANIMORPHS]™
titles by K.A. Applegate:

ANIMORPHS™

The Android

K.A. Applegate

AN
APPLE
PAPERBACK

SCHOLASTIC INC.
New York Toronto London Auckland Sydney

No part of this publication may be reproduced in whole or in part, or stored in a retrieval system, or transmitted in any form or by any means, electronic, mechanical, photocopying, recording, or otherwise, without written permission of the publisher. For information regarding permission, write to Scholastic Inc., 555 Broadway, New York, NY 10012.

ISBN 0-590-99730-0

12 11 10 9 8 7 6 5 4 3 2   7 8 9/9 0 1 2/0

Printed in the U.S.A.   40

First Scholastic printing, September 1997

For Erek King, and all the fans

And for Michael

The Android

Even the book morphs!
Flip the pages
and check it out!

CHAPTER 1

My name is Marco.

People call me Marco the Magnificent. Marvelous Marco. The Amazing Marco.

And of course, all the girls just call me . . . gorgeous. Okay, maybe I've never actually *heard* anyone call me gorgeous, but I am confident that someone, somewhere, must have called me gorgeous at some point.

Or not.

But definitely cute. I've heard "cute" with my own ears.

And I'll soon be hearing it a lot more because I've made a major change. I've cut my hair. Or at least my stylist, Charise, cut it for me. That's right, Charise. And according to Charise, my

1

cuteness quotient has risen from a nine to a definite ten.

Anyway, where was I? Oh, yes. I was telling you that my name is Marco. I can't tell you my last name. I forgot it.

No, not really, I'm kidding. I know my last name. I'm just not going to tell you. And I'm not going to tell you the complete names of my friends or where I live.

What I *will* tell you is the truth. All except for that part about "magnificent" and "marvelous." Everything else I tell you will be true. I know it will seem incredible. But it will be the absolute truth.

Let's start with the reason why I won't tell you my last name: I have enemies. We all sorta do. But these guys are very powerful, very dangerous enemies. Not like the guy in your class who keeps calling you "dork-wad." And if they knew who I was, I'd be dead so fast I wouldn't even know I was dead. The Yeerks don't play games. The Yeerks don't worry about pity or kindness. They don't care that I'm just a kid. The Yeerks plan to enslave or destroy the entire human race. They won't hesitate to roll right over little old me.

The Yeerks aren't just *my* enemies, though. They are the enemies of every human being. The enemies of Earth itself. And they are everywhere.

They're a parasitic species. Think tapeworms.

That's what they are, when you get right down to it: intelligent tapeworms.

They are slugs, just a few inches long. They enter the human body through the ear canal. Once inside, they flatten themselves out and wrap themselves around your brain. They squeeze into all the folds and wrinkles of your brain and tie into your thoughts.

They take over. They make you into what we call a Controller. A human machine. A body whose own, true mind is shattered and helpless.

That's the special horror of the Yeerks. They don't just take over your mind and eliminate you. You continue to be aware. You continue to be conscious. You sit there in your own head watching the Yeerk open your memory, watching the Yeerk fool your friends and family, watching the Yeerk turn the people you love into the same kind of slave you've become.

You try to move your hand, but you can't. You try to make your mouth speak, but you can't. You don't even control what your eyes look at. That's what it's like.

My mother is one of them. A Controller.

For a long time, we thought she had died. I believed she had drowned. But I learned later that she was still alive.

A very powerful Yeerk had taken her body. I don't even know how long she was a Controller

3

before she disappeared. I don't know how many times her good-night kiss was the action of a Yeerk trying to pass as a human.

She is Visser One now. A Visser is a sort of Yeerk warlord or general. Visser One launched the secret invasion of Earth. Visser Three is now in charge.

Visser One, in my mother's head, took off after faking her death by drowning. She's somewhere now . . . maybe millions of miles away.

No one knows about my mom but me and my best friend, Jake. I don't want the others to know. I don't want their pity.

The Yeerks are here. Everywhere. Not just my mother, but maybe yours, too. Maybe your teacher, maybe your best friend, maybe everyone around you. When you get together with family and friends, you may be the only one in the room who is not a Controller.

That's why we fight them. We Animorphs.

I made up that word, by the way. Pretty cool, huh? Animorphs. Just popped into my head. Animal morpher.

See, not every alien in the universe is a Yeerk. The universe has its heroes, too. It was one dying, doomed Andalite who gave us our power to acquire the DNA of any animal and then to become that animal.

His name was Elfangor. He, and a lot of other

4

Andalites, died trying to save Earth from the Yeerks.

So for him, and for all the people of Earth, we fight, hoping to slow the Yeerks down enough so that the Andalites will have a chance to come again and save us all.

Who is "we"? Well, there's me, Marco the Magnificent.

Then, there's Rachel-who-thinks-she's-*Xena: Warrior Princess.* And there's Tobias, the Bird-boy. And Cassie, the tree-hugger. And Ax, our resident Andalite.

And of course, our fearless leader, my boy, Jake.

My way-too-serious best friend Jake.

Responsible, practically adult Jake.

Jake, who grinds my nerves with his total re-fusal to just have a good time.

"Look," I said to Jake, "it's not a crime or anything. There is absolutely no law against dogs going to outdoor concerts. They don't have a ticket for dogs."

"You know, Marco, the point of morphing is not for us to get into concerts," Jake said.

We were walking down one of the streets of our subdivision. We'd shot some hoops down at the outdoor basketball court, and now Jake was dribbling the ball as we walked.

"Nine Inch Nails. Alanis. Offspring," I said.

5

He stopped and stared at me. "Marco?"

"Yeah?"

"What happened to your hair, man?"

"You're just noticing? Looks cool, huh?"

Jake just stared. "Offspring?" he asked. "You're sure Offspring will be there?"

I could see him weakening. He was dribbling slower. "I hear they are so great live. They kick. They dominate. They crush all opposition under foot. They rule. They —"

"Marco, after I've criticized Rachel and Cassie for using morphing for personal reasons, I can't just —"

"Who's going to tell them?" I argued. I ran my fingers through my new, shorter hair. It *was* cool-looking. I wasn't even going to pay attention to the way Jake just stared at it. It looked *cool*.

"I'd be a hypocrite," Jake said.

I thought for a moment. "You know, Jake . . . I have long suspected that Alanis may be a Controller. And, as a Controller, think of the damage she could do by leading young, impressionable kids like us astray. Oh, I hate to even think of it! We have a duty, Jake. We have a sacred *duty* to go to that concert and to find out once and for all whether any of these major stars are Controllers."

Jake smiled his slow smile. "That is easily the most pathetic excuse you have ever come up with."

I laughed. "Get serious. I've come up with lots of more pathetic excuses than that."

We were almost at Jake's house, so we stopped. Jake's brother Tom is one of *them* — a Controller. We don't talk inside his house.

"You know," Jake said, "the only possible way I could go along with this is if I found out *you* were going to this thing anyway. Then, see, I'd have to go along — reluctantly — just to watch your back."

Jake may be responsible and all, but he isn't a total forty-year-old.

I grinned. "Jake, I'm going to this concert, whether you like it or not."

"Then I guess I'd better go, just to cover your butt," Jake said. "You'll have to figure out how to cover that hair."

I made a face. "Real funny."

"I thought so," Jake said, grinning at his own wit. "I'm going to morph Homer, I guess. You're right. Dog is the way to go. No one will even think anything about us being there, since there are always dogs at outdoor stuff. And dog hearing is great. You need to acquire a dog morph."

"Already have," I said smugly. "An Irish setter. Girls love Irish setters. Heh, heh, heh."

I laughed my "evil" laugh and gave Jake a look, and he laughed, too.

There are these moments in your life that

7

seem totally innocent at first, you know? Like normal everyday life. But then it's like you stepped off a cliff, and before you know it you're falling. Suddenly you realize your innocent little decision has gone spinning out of control.

I had decided to sneak into a concert. I had not decided to uncover one of the greatest secrets of human history, or become the person who would decide the fate of an entire race.

I just wanted to hear some music.

It should have been no big deal.

CHAPTER 2

There are a couple of big problems with morphing. First of all, there's the two-hour time limit. If you stay in morph for more than two hours, you stay forever.

Second, there is the fact that all of the animal's basic instincts come along with the body. Sometimes when you jump into that animal brain it's like grabbing onto a power line.

Finally, there is the total creepiness factor. I mean, major, Stephen-King-meets-Ann-Rice creepy.

The concert was taking place at this big outdoor arena that's at one end of the city park. We needed a private place to morph, but that turned out not to be so easy. There were people everywhere. Thousands of people. Kids in black T-shirts. Displaced Deadheads with little granny sunglasses and dreadlocks. Parental units carrying babies and trying to look cool in their Dockers. And hardcore punk rockers with pierced everythings.

Across from the park there was this little street with coffee shops and restaurants and an ecology bookstore. There were alleys behind the restaurants, and we headed there.

Down one alley we found a little dead-end area stuffed with Dumpsters.

"Wonderful," Jake muttered. "The two of us and the garbage. This is already fun."

"Come on, let's do it," I said. I was impatient. I could hear a warm-up band racing through a power set.

"You haven't morphed a dog before, have you?" Jake asked me.

"No."

He smiled. "Don't get *too* happy," he said.

I didn't really pay any attention to him. I looked around and saw some hippie girls walking by. They couldn't see us. I removed my outer clothing and stripped down to my morphing suit. I stuffed my clothes and shoes into the bag Jake and I had brought along and shoved it behind the Dumpster.

I focused on the dog I had acquired. I saw it in my mind. And as I focused, I felt the changes begin.

I've morphed much weirder things than dogs. But every morph is strange. Every morph is unpredictable. You really never know how it's going to go.

I expected the first thing to be fur. It wasn't. The first thing that happened was the tail. I felt it just sort of spurt out of the base of my spine.

I turned to look back over my shoulder. "Oh, guh-ross!"

The tail was sticking out. But it had no fur yet. It was just this kind of grayish, chicken-skinned whip.

I looked back at Jake. His face was bulging out like something was trying to climb out of his mouth. At the same time my own muzzle started to grow. There was a weird grinding sound from inside my head as the bones of my jaw stretched outward.

I felt an itching in my mouth as my teeth grew bigger and rearranged themselves.

I saw my fingers shrink up inside my hands. At the same time, the little stubs of fingers grew these gray-black nails. My palms became thick and calloused.

I felt the bones in my legs and arms stretching, changing directions, and I began to grow slightly smaller. Suddenly, I couldn't stand up anymore. I fell forward onto my calloused pads.

Only then did the fur begin to grow. It was a good thing, too. I was one ugly animal without fur. The reddish fur sprouted quickly, like the world's fastest grass. It just seemed to explode out of my skin, long and silky.

<Cool,> I said to Jake in thought-speak. <Check out this fur. Every girl in that concert is going to want to pet me.>

He said something back to me, but right then the dog senses kicked in.

I've morphed a wolf, so I was prepared. I knew the hearing would be amazing. I knew the sense of smell would be incredible.

But what I didn't expect was the dog's mind. It was not like the wolf. The wolf was a cool, intelligent, ruthless killer.

The dog was just a big goof.

You remember that old song, "Girls Just Wanna Have Fun"? That could be the theme song for dogs. Dogs just want to have fun.

That's what fooled me. The Irish setter's brain didn't feel like some strange animal. It felt like it was just tapping into a part of my own mind. It was a perfect fit with the goofball part of my own brain.

I looked over at Jake through my slightly dim dog vision. He had become his dog, Homer. I lolled out my tongue and panted. Jake/Homer panted right back at me.

"RUFF!" I barked, for no reason. I did a little dance. Sort of like I was going to run away, but then I stopped suddenly and crouched down on my front legs and grinned like an idiot at Jake.

I was inviting him to play.

I tore off down the alley at a run.

<Marco, wait up!>

<Catch me! Hah-hah! Like you even could!>

I scrabbled away at top speed, my nails clicking on the concrete, my floppy ears flying, my tail held high and wagging.

I raced down the alleyway, totally ignoring the rich, wondrous smells of rotting garbage.

I turned toward the park and raced across the street. Jake fell back, caught up in a small knot of people.

SCRRREEEEECCCCHHH!

A car slammed on its brakes and missed me by a couple of feet. A couple of feet! I mean, if the driver had been one millisecond slower to hit the brakes, I'd have been roadkill. But my complete dog-brain reaction to that near-death experience was, "Cool! I smell something!"

I'm totally serious. The fact that I smelled

13

some other dog's pee on a curb was about ten thousand times more interesting to my dog brain than the squealing car was.

The driver got out and started yelling. I gave him a happy dog grin and trotted on my way.

<Marco! Would you wait up?>

Suddenly I was surrounded by people. But they were totally different from the people I'd seen before when I was still human.

For one thing, I wasn't really *looking* at these people. I was *smelling* them. What they looked like was so totally not important. But the smells!

I smelled sweat, I smelled shampoo, I smelled bad breath, I smelled what they had been eating, I smelled what they had stepped in, I smelled laundry detergent, I smelled everyone they had touched or shaken hands with.

And I could smell all their animals. The humans might as well have been wearing big neon signs that said I OWN A DOG, or I HAVE CATS. I could not only smell who owned dogs, I could smell whether the dogs were male or female, young or old, fixed or not. Just by sniffing the people walking past, I knew if their dogs ate canned or dry food.

I mean, when you hook up to that dog nose it's like you've been walking around with cotton balls up your nostrils all your life and suddenly you take them out and wow! Wow! You're into a whole new experience of life.

I'd been a wolf in the forest. Now it was like I was a wolf in civilization. The information from my nose was so complex. So full, so rich, so enjoyable.

"Hey, boy!" someone said. A girl! I was sure she was a girl. But was she a cute girl? I tried to make my dog eyes focus, but it was like sight was just irrelevant. I could see pretty well, but my dog brain was way too busy smelling and hearing. I did notice the scent of patchouli oil, though.

The girl reached out a hand and stroked my head. Instantly a warm wave of pleasure washed over me. Then she scratched behind my ear.

This was almost too good. This was sublime. This was probably the best thing I'd ever felt in my life.

I think I could have just stood there and let her scratch behind my ear forever. But then she was joined by a guy — a guy who owned a cat, incidentally — and she started in on my ribs. I lay down and rolled on my side. The scratching of my ribs felt like tickling. I was so happy. I was beyond happy.

See, dog happy isn't like human happy. Human happiness always has this little voice in the back of your mind going, "Don't be *too* happy.

15

Keep your guard up. Something bad could still happen."

But dog happy is just pure, distilled essence of happiness. I just lolled my wet tongue out and slapped my tail against the grass, and then it started. My leg started going all on its own.

"Hah, I love it when dogs do that," the guy said. "That's so funny!"

His girlfriend scratched away on my ribs and my back leg just motored away, out of control, and I was in heaven. That's when Jake found me.

<That's nice, Marco,> Jake said. <Very dignified. What's next? You going to lick yourself?>

"Oh, it's another dog," the girl said. "He's even cuter!" She leaned forward to pet Jake.

That brought me to my senses. No way was Jake a cuter dog than me.

<Okay, okay, that's enough playing around,> I said. <Come on, Jake. Let's get closer to the stage.>

We took off, tails wagging, leaving the nice hippie couple behind.

<See? I told you, Marco. Don't get too happy. A happy dog is almost *too* happy.>

<Why not?> I asked, a little wistfully. <Why not just get happy?>

Then something stunning happened. There had been no music for a few minutes, and all at once, Offspring climbed onstage and unloaded.

16

They ripped into a song and I cowered a little. The impact on my dog ears was shocking. But it wasn't just that it was so loud. It was that I could hear everything. Everything.

<Hey! I can understand the lyrics now,> I said.

<Cool,> Jake answered.

We trotted closer, into a thickening crowd of humans. The smells were just overwhelming. And not always in a good way.

Suddenly, I saw him. He was passing out flyers. He was walking through the crowd and passing out handbills.

A breeze caught one of the sheets and it fluttered to the ground in front of me. I forced my dog eyes to look at it. I couldn't read the fine print, but I could see the two big words at the top.

The Sharing.

The Sharing. The front organization for Controllers.

<Jake,> I said. <That guy. He's handing out flyers for The Sharing.>

<Yeah. You know what? Does he look familiar, or is it just my imagination?>

He had brown hair, just a little over his ears. He was maybe five feet tall, but he managed to look taller. A slightly shorter version of Jake, strong and confident-looking. <Yes, he's familiar.

17

His name's Erek King. He transferred out of our school like a year ago.>

Erek was coming closer, smiling and handing out flyers to anyone who would take one.

He knelt down and smiled at me. He reached out to pet me, but I pulled back. Erek shrugged and walked on his way, handing out flyers.

<Jake, did you notice that?>

<Oh, yeah,> he said. <Definitely.>

<Oh, man,> I said. <There is something very, very wrong with Erek.>

CHAPTER 3

"He didn't smell," I said.

"What do you mean, he didn't smell?" Rachel demanded.

"I mean that he didn't *smell*. He had picked up some odors off other people, off the ground, off dogs, whatever, but he had no smell himself. None. Like a black hole of smell. Like nothing there, nobody home."

It was later that same evening. Jake and I had left the concert shortly after encountering Erek. We'd called a meeting, and now everyone except Ax was in Cassie's barn.

Cassie's barn is actually the Wildlife Rehabilitation Center. It's a sort of hospital for messed-up wild animals. Cassie's parents are both

19

veterinarians. Her mom works at the Gardens, this big combination zoo and amusement park.

Her dad (with a lot of help from Cassie) takes in every sick or injured wild animal they come across. The barn is lined with wire cages filled with raccoons, foxes, opossums, eagles, rabbits, geese, badgers, crows, squirrels . . . I mean, you name it. It's animal central.

"Maybe you just didn't notice it," Rachel suggested.

"Rachel, you've been in wolf morph," Jake said. "You know how good your sense of smell is? Well, the dog's sense of smell is almost that good."

Rachel shook her head. That's what she does when she's frustrated.

She was standing in the middle of the barn floor, looking immaculate, as usual. Rachel is one of those girls from the cover of *Seventeen*. Beautiful, fashionable, way too tall, far too many bright white teeth, massive quantities of very clean blond hair. But beneath all that fashionable clothing and perfectly applied makeup there is a sword-swinging Amazon warrior just trying to break out.

Rachel's like one of those terrible elf-maidens in Tolkien's *The Lord of the Rings* — beautiful and dangerous.

Jake is her cousin and Cassie is her best

friend. Cassie actually experiences normal human emotions like fear and doubt. I approve of this because I sure experience plenty of fear and doubt myself. I've experienced more fear and doubt since I became an Animorph than most people experience in about ten lifetimes.

Cassie has never met a dress she liked. She does not subscribe to *Teen* or *YM*. She's much more likely to buy a magazine like *Smelly Animals of America*. You know, the kind of magazine that would have articles like "How to Give Suppositories to Raccoons," or "Let's Examine Owl Vomit!"

If you want to picture Cassie, think of a short, cute girl with very short black hair, wearing overalls and big muddy boots and looking totally capable of giving a tetanus shot to an angry bear.

Cassie is our animal expert, and our resident ecology nut. I'd say she likes animals better than she likes people, except that she really likes Jake. As in *likes*.

Actually, she and Jake *like* each other, although neither of them will admit it, of course. The only time they'll act that way is when we're about twelve seconds away from doing something insanely dangerous. Then they'll kind of give each other these pathetic sad looks.

It's so lame.

The last original member of our group was

perched in the high rafters overhead. Tobias had his talons sunk deep into the wood to give himself a firm hold. And with his hooked beak he was preening the feathers of his right wing.

Tobias is a red-tailed hawk. That's what he's been since he stayed too long in morph. He lives as a hawk now, mostly. I mean, he hunts and eats like a hawk. Not that he has much choice. I don't think the school is really interested in a Hawk-boy as a student.

Tobias lives in the woods, along with Ax. Ax is an Andalite, the brother of Elfangor, and the only free Andalite within a billion miles of Earth.

Ax doesn't come to the meetings, usually. He has a human morph, but he doesn't like to overuse it. Besides, he basically figures Jake is his "prince," and he'll do whatever his prince tells him has to be done.

So, that's our little group. Rachel, standing in the middle of the room, looking like someone was shining a spotlight on her. Jake, pacing back and forth and looking far too intense. Cassie, cradling a duck in her arms while she changed its bandage. Tobias, preening his feathers and looking around with that eternal hawk glare. And me, lolling back on a bale of hay.

"Shh," Jake said suddenly. "I thought I heard something."

<It's just a squirrel up on the roof,> Tobias assured him in thought-speak.

"You sure?" Jake asked.

Tobias stopped preening and stared down at Jake. His hawk stare grew even more intense. <Am I *sure*? I *do* know what a squirrel sounds like.>

Jake nodded and looked a little embarrassed. Hawks not only have amazingly good eyes, their hearing is better than human, too. And Tobias knows the sounds that prey make. He has to. Asking Tobias if he recognizes squirrel sounds would be like asking Einstein if he knows how to add two plus two.

I tried to bring us all back to the topic. "So, what does it mean if a kid doesn't smell like a human?"

"There are plenty of times when you don't smell human," Rachel said with a smirk. "But then, maybe that's because you have a small monkey living on top of your head."

Cassie made a snorking sound as she tried not to laugh.

"Next time you decide to get a haircut, talk to me first," Rachel said.

I ignored them both. We had important business, and I was not going to lower myself to trading insults with Rachel. Besides, I couldn't think of any.

"He doesn't smell, *and* he's handing out flyers for The Sharing," I said.

"He must be connected to the Yeerks," Rachel said with a shrug.

"But how?" Cassie asked. She was pushing the duck back into his cage. "I mean, Yeerks infest various species — humans, Hork-Bajir, Taxxons. But that doesn't change the fact that a human with a Yeerk in his head should still smell like a human. You know?"

"Chapman is a Controller. He still smells human," I pointed out. "And by the way, I can't believe I'm even talking about how the vice principal smells."

Jake shrugged. "I guess we need to find out what's going on with Erek."

"But how do we find him?" I asked. "Infiltrate a meeting of The Sharing?"

<I could do surveillance of his school,> Tobias said.

"Or maybe we could go back to where the concert was and look for clues," Rachel said. Then she winced. "Wow, that sounded so Nancy Drew."

"Maybe Ax can try and tap into the Internet and get past all the security buffers and locate him," I suggested.

Cassie held up her hand like she was asking a

question at school. "Those are all fine plans, but how about if we just look him up in the phone book?"

We all just stared at her.

"Or we could just look him up in the phone book," Jake said sheepishly.

Cassie headed for the house to get a phone book.

"You know, she is just not getting the whole superhero thing," I said to Jake. "Does Wolverine look things up in the phone book? Does Spider-man? I don't think so."

"Yeah, well, Wolverine has a big advantage over us," Rachel said dryly. "He's not real."

Then she snapped her fingers. "That's what that hair of yours reminds me of: a wolverine. I knew it was something."

"Oh, yeah?" I shot back. "Well, how about your . . . your . . ."

"My what?" Rachel asked coolly, with the absolute confidence of a girl who never looked less than perfect.

"Your tallness," I said lamely. "You're . . . tall. Way tall."

Somehow this brilliant comeback did not cause Rachel to break down in tears.

Cassie came back carrying the white pages, already open to the "K's." "There are twenty-seven 'Kings' listed. But you said he transferred to Truman, so there are maybe six 'Kings' that are in that part of town."

"We work our way down the list," I said. "Although he still could have an unlisted phone."

"I can't hang out tonight," Jake said. "I have *got* to write that English paper."

"Here's a clue on the English paper. Don't say 'I have got to,'" I teased.

"I could go tomorrow, maybe," Rachel said. "But not tonight. My dad is in town just for tonight. He's taking me and my sisters to Planet Hollywood."

Cassie looked at me. "I'm free," she said.

<I'm good till it gets dark,> Tobias volunteered. Hawks aren't much use at night.

"Fine. Me and Cassie and Tobias till it gets dark," I said. "Shouldn't be too hard. Our mission: to find the boy who doesn't smell."

"Maybe he just showers a lot," Rachel said. "Did you think about that?"

CHAPTER 4

I saw Jake the following day in the school cafeteria.

I was wolfing down the Goo of the Day, drinking milk, and trying to write *my* English paper at warp speed. See, I kind of had some homework due, too. But I'd spent yesterday evening cruising around in owl morph looking for Erek's house.

"English paper?" Jake asked as he sat down across from me.

"Yeah."

He laughed. "You're good for me, Marco. Compared to you, I'm so responsible. You have a topic?"

I looked up at him and thumped my finger

27

down on the paper. "I've already written three pages. What do you mean, do I have a topic?"

But Jake knows me. "So," he said. "*Do* you have a topic?"

"A topic will . . . emerge. I'm going to just write until I discover a topic. The topic will rise from these pages. It will reveal itself to me. I just have to keep writing."

He nodded and made a face at the Goo of the Day on his tray. "This food is blue. Food should not be blue. Hey, here's a topic for you — the use of total bull in the writing of English papers."

I grinned. "I am the master of bull. Three pages so far and I haven't actually said a single thing."

"So. Did you guys happen to find our friend?"

I shot a glance left and then right. No one was seated near enough to overhear us. Besides, the cafeteria was so noisy from yelling and laughing and clashing dishes and scraping chairs that no one could hear much of anything.

"Yeah. We found out where he lives. Saw him through a window. Too bad, though. One of the other King residences we checked out had this girl living there who was amazing."

"You weren't window-peeping, I hope."

I gave Jake my best shocked-and-outraged look. "How could you even say that? What kind of person do you think I am?"

Jake nodded. "Cassie wouldn't let you, huh?"

"I *am* trying to write a paper here," I said.

"On the topic of . . . ?"

"On the topic of how to write a thousand words and say nothing. Zero. *Nada.* Squat."

Jake lowered his voice to just above a whisper. "We need to check Erek out. Definitely something wrong there."

I put down my pencil. "You mean get inside his house?"

Jake shrugged. "Not yet. Get Tobias to watch him when he's outside. But Tobias will need some help."

I shrugged and went back to my paper. "I'll help. I'll have plenty of time. I'm dropping out of school this afternoon. Right after the teacher gets done laughing at this paper."

"Topic — the use of rhetoric to obscure a lack of content," Jake said.

I froze. I looked up. "That's brilliant! It means the same as 'the use of total bull' . . . but it sounds so much better!"

"Eat your Goo. I gotta go."

He left and I saw him head over to the spot where Cassie was sitting.

It's one of our rules. We can never start looking like a "group." In school or in public places, we keep our distance. We only reveal the relationships that already existed before we became Animorphs.

29

I happened to see Chapman coming in through the door of the cafeteria. He grabbed some kid who was running and told him to slow down. Then he gazed around the room, looking for troublemakers, like any normal vice principal would.

But Chapman isn't normal. Chapman is a Controller. The Yeerk in his head is high-ranking enough to speak directly with Visser Three.

For about a second, Chapman's eyes locked on mine.

It was nothing. But it sent a shiver up my spine.

Chapman runs The Sharing. The flyers that Erek had been handing out at the concert had been about The Sharing.

Erek had never been some major friend of mine. He was just this kid I'd say hi to in the hallway. Except that he had been there for my mother's funeral.

A funeral without a body.

Some other kids from school had come, so I didn't think anything much about it. Still, it was a nice thing for him to do.

And now he was working for The Sharing.

The Sharing is a front organization for Controllers. On the surface, it's a sort of club. Kids join it and go on camp-outs and field trips and stuff. Adults join it and supposedly do business deals together and take weekends at ski resorts.

And probably most members of The Sharing never even know what's really going on. But the Controllers who run The Sharing are always on the lookout for some person with problems.

See, the Yeerks don't just spread by forcing themselves on people. A lot of people become Controllers by choice. I guess they want to feel like they're part of something bigger. Or maybe it's the secrecy they think is cool. I don't know.

All I know is that the Yeerks would rather have a voluntary host. They'd rather have you surrender your mind than have to take it by force.

They work you up slowly through the levels of The Sharing, till they decide you're ready. Then they make promises and tell you lies, and the next thing you know, you're a slave inside your own mind, all the more easily controlled because you *let* it happen.

I shoved the tray away from me and picked up my pencil again. I stared down at the paper. But I was seeing a funeral service. Singing. Flowers. Some priest talking about how great my mother had been. He hadn't even known my mother.

I remember turning around in my pew to look at the church. A lot of people had come. A lot of sad faces. A lot of tears. Most people just looking solemn because that's the way you had to look at a funeral.

Erek had been three rows back. He was wear-

31

ing a suit that was probably scratchy and uncomfortable. But he didn't look solemn. He looked angry. And he was shaking his head slowly, barely, from side to side, as if he was unconsciously disagreeing with everything the priest said.

At the time I figured he was mad because he had to dress up. I understood that.

And now Erek had reappeared. The boy who didn't smell human. The boy who worked for The Sharing.

"Well, Erek," I muttered under my breath, "we'll have to see about you. We will definitely have to see."

CHAPTER 5

There may be something in this world cooler than flying on your own wings, but I can't imagine what it is.

Rollerblading? Hah! Surfing? Big deal. Skydiving? Closer, but not halfway to actual flying.

Nothing is as cool as flying.

It was after school that same day. I'd finished the English paper exactly nine seconds before the teacher came around to collect it. Then I'd gone to history and been assigned another paper. That's the nature of school: It never really ends.

But finally the bell rang and blessed freedom! I was outta there and looking for a private place to morph. I wanted to check up on Erek. Remembering the funeral and all had made it seem even more important, although I wasn't sure I knew why.

I climbed up onto the roof of the gym. Of course, no one is supposed to go up there, but hey, it was for a good reason. I morphed into an osprey. It's a bird, a kind of hawk that usually lives right near the water.

I spread my broad wings and I flew away from school.

Tell me you haven't sat there in some boring class, while some teacher went on and on (and on and on) about how "x" equaled "y" but only if you multiplied it by pi, and wished you could just fly right out the window. Zoom! Good-bye!

Well, I can't fly right out of class because if I morphed in class there would be a lot of screaming and hysteria. But I can come close to doing it.

Kids were still piling onto the buses as I caught a nice little headwind and used it to go airborne. I zoomed high above all the kids heading for their buses, and all the teachers heading for their cars. People were just ovals of black, brown, blond, and red hair to me. That's mostly what a person looks like from a hundred feet up. A hair oval.

I have never felt as totally alive as when I'm in a hawk morph. Tobias doesn't have it all that bad, in some ways. There are so many worse animals to be.

I felt a thermal, a pillar of warm air, billow up beneath my wings and I went for it. Zoom! Like riding an elevator to the top floor! Up and up. The warm air currents swept me higher and higher.

<Yah-HAH!>

Now the hair ovals were just dots, and the buses were bright yellow toys pulling slowly away from the school.

But even from five hundred feet up in the air, as high as a fifty-story building, I could still see faces behind the school bus windows. With the osprey's eyes, it's like wearing binoculars.

I floated up there, wings spread wide, my tail fanned out to catch every bit of lift, my talons tucked back against the underside of my body. Air rushed over the leading edge of my wings, making a slight fluttering sound. Wind flowed over my streamlined head, and I kept my hooked beak pointed forward to maintain every ounce of momentum.

I rode that thermal as high as it would carry me. I'd learned that from Tobias. See, the thermal will give you altitude for almost no effort, and you can turn that altitude into distance. It's like soaring to the top of a mountain, then skiing down the slopes in whatever direction you want to go.

Still, it did eventually require some hard wing-flapping to get to Erek's neighborhood.

I spotted Tobias from far off, when he would have been invisible to any human eye. He was riding the wind, just like me. Maybe with a little more style, since he'd had so much more experience.

When I got close to enough to try thought-speak, I called to him.

<Tobias? Can you hear me?>

<I can hear you and see you, Marco. I've been watching you for twenty minutes.>

<No way. I just spotted you.>

<You have to know what to look for, Marco. By the way . . . when I count to three, you need to bank a very sharp, very fast left turn.>

<Turn? Why?>

<Just do it! One. Two. THREE!>

I raised one wing, lowered the other, skewed my tail, and cut a sudden, sharp left.

FWOOOOM!

<Aaaahhhhh!>

A missile blew past me, doing what seemed like a thousand miles an hour! Only it wasn't coming from the ground upward, it had fallen from the sky down! And this missile had gray feathers.

The wind from its passing nearly knocked me off balance. It was half a mile away, down and south, by the time I could even try to think about focusing.

I saw swept-back, slate-gray wings and a tight tail. It was diving away from me so fast it made me look like I was standing still.

<What the . . . What was *that*?!> I yelled.

<Heh, heh, heh. Welcome to my world,> Tobias said. <That's a peregrine falcon. You know, like Jake's morph. They usually prefer to knock off a tasty pigeon or the occasional duck. It must have been the way you were flying. He probably thought you were a big old clumsy duck.>

<Jeez. What did I ever do to make him mad?>

<Shake it off,> Tobias advised. <He missed, right? I know that bird. He's not as good as he thinks he is. He's taken a shot at me before. He must be hungry.>

Suddenly flying didn't seem nearly as fun. <Yeah. I'll shake it off. That should be easy, since I'll be shaking for at least another hour.>

<It's not all just about riding thermals,> Tobias said dryly. <Come on, you want to see our boy Erek?>

I moved closer to Tobias. Much closer. This was his world up here in the air. He knew what he was doing. <By the way, thanks,> I said.

<Always remember to look up,> Tobias advised. <The danger is usually above you. But on a lighter note . . . that's Erek right there. He walks home from his school. See him? Coming to the corner?>

I spotted the oval of hair below me. <Yeah, I see him.>

<I watched him this morning on his way in. I watched him play soccer during gym —>

<They play soccer? They play soccer during gym? Man, we never get to play soccer.>

<Now he's heading home. I'm going to let you take over because I am hungry. And I am also bored with looking at the top of his head.>

<Did he do anything weird or different?>

<He scored a goal in soccer. Does that count?>

<Hey. Look.> I had noticed three guys closing in behind Erek. Something in the way they moved caught my attention. From high up, it looked almost as if they were hunting Erek.

<Hmmm. That's not good,> Tobias said.

We both spilled air from our wings and dived, wanting a closer look. I could see the face of one of the guys behind Erek. It was an expression I had seen before: the idiot, giggling sneer of a bully.

Suddenly, the guys raced forward. Erek spotted them and started to run.

It was a street on the edge of a development. There was a lot of traffic to Erek's left and a stone wall to his right. The stone wall ended about fifty yards away, where it opened for the entrance to the subdivision.

<If this guy is a Controller, these punks are making a serious mistake,> I said. <They may get him today, but they might regret it later.>

<Maybe I'll just give that one jerk a little talon haircut,> Tobias said.

Tobias hates bullies. Back when he was human, he was the kid most likely to be pounded on. Jake met Tobias when Tobias's head was just about to be flushed in the toilet. Naturally, Jake helped him.

<Tobias, I don't think —> I started to say, but it was too late. Tobias was in a stoop and aiming for the biggest guy's head.

It all happened in a flash.

Erek ran. He tripped. He sprawled forward, out into the street. He slammed into the broad side of a passing bus.

WHAM! I could hear the impact from up in the air.

And then . . .

And then . . . for just a second, Erek wasn't there anymore. Something else was where he had been.

Something that seemed to be made of patches of steel and milk-white plastic.

Then, in the next split second, Erek was back. A normal boy, lying winded on the sidewalk.

The bullies ran off. The bus driver never even noticed and drove on.

39

Tobias opened his wings and nearly stopped in midair.

<Did you *see* that?> Tobias asked.

<Yeah. I sure did.>

<What was that?>

<I don't know,> I said. <But I know what it *wasn't*. It wasn't human.>

CHAPTER 6

<⫴e need to talk to Ax,> I said to Tobias.

<Definitely. That was not human. That was seriously not human.>

<So you did see it, right? I'm not crazy?>

<Yes, you're crazy. But I *did* see it,> Tobias said. <Very weird.>

Below us, Erek climbed up off the sidewalk, dusted himself off like nothing had happened, and resumed walking toward home.

<Hang a right,> Tobias said. <We'll get some good updrafts off the road. Whatever your friend Erek is, I don't think he's from around here.>

We flew hard and fast toward home. Tobias split off to round up Ax. I demorphed and headed home to check in with my dad and let him know I still existed. Then I called Jake.

I got Tom instead.

"Hey, Tom. Is Jake around there?"

"I don't know. JAKE!" he yelled. "He said he's coming."

"Cool."

"Haven't seen you around here much," Tom said. "Keeping busy?"

I felt a little chill. It's weird, talking to Controllers when you know that's what they are. It was Tom's voice, and it acted like Tom, but it wasn't Tom. Tom was cowering helplessly in a corner of his own mind.

I was talking to a Yeerk.

"Yeah, I guess so," I said.

"Uh-huh. We're going up to the lake, do some waterskiing."

"You and Jake?"

"Yeah, right. No, me and The Sharing. You know Jake's too much of a social misfit to join," Tom said with a totally human, big-brother laugh of derision. "It's just that we have too many girls going and not enough guys."

A lie, of course. A lie that was supposed to entice me. Why was Tom suddenly trying to get me interested in The Sharing again? He quickly gave me the answer.

"So. I heard your dad was back at work. That's cool."

"Yeah, I guess so," I said. My father had gone

through a bad time after my mom "died." Now he was back at work. He's an engineer, but he's heavily involved in computers, too. He had been working with the new observatory on ways to design software that would aim the telescopes better.

He was also working on some projects he couldn't even talk about. Projects I figured must involve the military.

"You could bring your dad," Tom said as casually as he could. "I mean, not like anyone wants their fathers along, usually, right? But I mean, maybe he's ready to get back out there in the world and all. The Sharing is a good place to make business connections, you know?"

"Yeah, I'll ask him," I said.

"Do that, okay? Your dad could probably use some down time to relax, take it easy, meet some people."

So. They were after my father now. I felt something burning inside me, like I'd taken a gulp of lava. I wanted to reach right through the phone and take a baseball bat to the evil creature in Tom's head.

"Here's Jake," Tom said. There was a scuffling sound as he handed the phone off. Then Jake's voice.

"Hey, Marco. What's up?"

I went off. "What's up?! What's *up*? Those

scumbags are after my father, that's what's up! How do you live with that? How do you look at that piece of crap every day? He's all like, 'Bring your dad to The Sharing, do a father–son bonding thing, and oh, by the way, would you mind if we stuck a —'"

"Shut up," Jake hissed.

I shut up. But my hand was squeezing the receiver so hard I could have snapped it. Jake let me calm down for a minute. He made "uh-huh" noises in the phone, like he was listening to me talking. He made a couple of laughing sounds. I guess Tom wasn't far away from the phone.

I knew Jake was right. We don't talk secrets over the phone. There's no way of knowing who might be listening in.

"Okay, I'm cool," I said. I wasn't cool, but I was under control again.

"That sounds good to me," Jake said, still pretending to have a conversation.

"We have to get together," I said. "It's a nice day out."

That was the signal that we should meet in the woods.

"Okay. Later," Jake said casually.

He hung up.

I took a couple of deep breaths. Then I took a couple more.

The Yeerks had taken my mother. They weren't

getting my father. Before that happened I'd tell him everything. Before I'd let that happen I'd take Tom down, no matter what Jake said.

I'd take Tom, I'd take Chapman, I'd take every Controller I knew of before I'd let them have my father. I had power. Deadly animals lived inside me. Their DNA swam with my own.

I could feel the rage flowing through me, the blind, violent rage that became little films in my head — little head-movies of revenge and destruction. I pictured the things I would do to Tom . . . to Chapman . . . someday even to Visser Three. I would do terrible things to them. Terrible, violent things.

It was a sick feeling. It was sick, and I knew it, and yet I ran those images over and over in my head.

Rage is addictive, you know. I guess it's sorta like a drug. Anger and hatred get you high. They get you high, but like any addiction, they hollow you out and tear you down and eat you alive.

I guess I knew all that. But all I could think of was that they were *not* getting my father.

So I ran the scenes of violence over and over in my head. I rode that rush of fury till at last it burned itself out and left me feeling empty and beaten.

45

CHAPTER 7

I hooked up with Jake and the two of us rode our bikes to Cassie's farm. He didn't say anything about my conversation with Tom. Jake knew how I felt. We've all felt it before.

From Cassie's farm we walked across the fields to the edge of the forest. There's a place we meet there, deep enough in the trees that no one is likely to see us.

Rachel and Cassie were already there. Cassie was on her knees in the pine needles, looking into a burrow hole. I have no idea what was in there, but she seemed fascinated. Rachel was sitting on a fallen log.

"Tobias is off finding Ax," Rachel said as we approached.

"I think there are three of them," Cassie said. I guess she was talking about whatever was in that burrow.

"So? What's the big panic?" Rachel asked.

Before Jake or I could answer, I heard something crashing through the brush.

He leaped into view, sailing over the log Rachel was sitting on. Aximili-Esgarrouth-Isthill.

"Hey, Ax," I said. "Very dramatic entrance."

Of course, any appearance by Ax was going to be dramatic. Ax is an Andalite. The only Andalite to survive when their Dome ship was destroyed by the Yeerks in high orbit. He's an alien.

You know how on *Star Trek* the aliens are always just humans with a little nose putty and some bad outfits? But they basically look human and act human and speak English?

Well, Ax isn't like that. You take one look at Ax and you know he isn't from around here.

Picture a sort of big, blue-and-tan deer. Only instead of a deer neck and head, you have a semi-human chest with two weak arms, topped by a head that is definitely unusual. Ax has no mouth and four eyes. Two of his eyes are in the usual location, but his other two eyes are mounted on stalks on top of his head. The stalk eyes can aim totally independently. Ax can look right at you with his two main eyes, and still be looking behind him with one stalk and off to the right with his other stalk.

It's kind of unsettling, till you get used to it.

But not nearly as unsettling as his tail. The tail makes you think scorpion. It curves up and over, so that the razor-sharp blade-tip is usually poised somewhere above his sloping shoulders.

That tail is fast and dangerous. Very fast, very dangerous. Basically, Ax could slice-and-dice a human into bite-sized chunks in about two seconds.

Fortunately, Ax is on our side.

<Hello, Prince Jake. Hello Marco, Rachel. Cassie? Did you lose something?>

Cassie stood up. Then, as an afterthought, she brushed off her knees. "Baby opossums," she said, by way of explanation. "Too big for the pouch, not ready to leave the den."

"Don't tell Tobias," I said. "He'll eat 'em."

<I already know about them,> Tobias said.

I looked up in surprise. He was in the tree above me. I hadn't heard him arrive.

Cassie shrugged. "Tobias is a hawk. He has a right to be a hawk." Then she looked up at Tobias and smiled. "Of course, they are awfully cute."

<Oh, man,> Tobias groaned. <Okay, okay, this litter is off-limits. Happy now?>

"You're a sweetheart, Tobias," Cassie said.

<We should move while we talk,> Tobias suggested. <There are some kids playing soldier just about three hundred yards west. Let's stay well out of range.>

We all started walking east, and Tobias went up again to scout ahead for any danger.

"Okay, Marco," Jake said after a few minutes. "This is your party. What's up?"

I told them all what Tobias and I had seen. Tobias came back and added some details. Then I looked to Ax.

"So, Ax, you're the official alien. What does this sound like to you?"

Ax turned his head toward me, making eye contact with his main eyes. <Marco? Something has happened to your hair. I believe it has become shorter. Are you suffering from some sort of illness?>

"That does it!" I yelled, as the others all broke up giggling. "It'll grow out, all right? It'll grow out. Besides, it's easier to take care of. Man! I make one little change!"

<Have I said something wrong?> Ax wondered.

"No," Jake assured him. "Not at all. Marco is just a little sensitive. Go ahead, Ax. What do you think about this Erek person?"

<I do not know. It . . . it doesn't sound like any species I know of.>

"What? Dude, you're the expert on aliens," I pointed out.

<Marco, even we Andalites don't know every species in the galaxy.>

I swear he sounded embarrassed. Although since he was using thought-speak, maybe "sounded" isn't the right word.

"You don't recognize the description?" Jake asked.

<No.>

"The way you guys describe it, it sounds more like a robot or something," Rachel ventured. "But how does it pass for human?"

<Oh, that is technologically possible,> Ax said, relieved to be able to add something to our speculation. <It's probably a holographic projection. Like your primitive TV, only three-dimensional.>

"*Primitive* TV? Hey, we have cable at my house," I said. Ax didn't think it was funny, but Cassie smiled.

Tobias swooped low over our heads and came to rest on a branch. <So when Erek gets hit by the bus, he drops the hologram for just a split second.>

<The power supply may have been interrupted or overloaded,> Ax suggested. <But that's the interesting question: What power supply? It

would take a great deal of power to maintain such a hologram, hour after hour, day after day.>

"Hey, maybe Erek is nuclear-powered," I said.

Ax laughed. Then I guess he realized I wasn't joking. <I don't think nuclear power is likely,> he said, still sort of giggling like I was the primitive moron of the universe. <I think it would take something much more advanced.>

"Is there any way to see through this hologram?" Cassie asked.

"We could hit him with something as big as a bus," Rachel suggested.

"Now, there's a classic Rachel suggestion," I said with a laugh. I was feeling better, hanging with my friends.

"Marco found out The Sharing is having a little waterskiing thing up at the lake," Jake said. He bit his lip and added, "Tom told him. Erek is in The Sharing. He'll probably be there, too. Perfect chance for us to get a good look at him. That's the 'where.' Now we just need the 'how.'"

Ax thought for a moment as we ambled through the woods. <The hologram is meant to trick humans. It would be tuned for *human* sight. Hawk eyes are better than human, but still see similar wavelengths of light. Maybe a totally different sort of vision would be able to penetrate the hologram.>

My heart sank. I knew what was coming next. Some gross morph.

"Unusual vision is our specialty," Rachel said with a careless laugh. She slapped me on the back like life was just one big adventure.

Sometimes Rachel really grinds my nerves.

"No bugs, okay?" I said. "All I'm saying is, no more insect morphs. Is that too much to ask?"

CHAPTER 8

I guess it *was* too much to ask, as I found out a couple days later.

"What do you mean, we're going to draw straws?" I asked suspiciously.

"To see who morphs our new morph," Rachel said. "Ax is in, regardless. We need his expertise in aliens. One of us has to go in with him."

"What's the morph?" I asked suspiciously.

"Spider," Cassie said.

We were at Cassie's barn. It was Saturday morning. On Friday I'd found out I'd gotten a "B" on my English paper. How cool is that? I'd stayed up watching TV with my dad and been late for this meeting.

This was the kind of insanity they cooked up when I wasn't there.

"Excuse me? I must have something wrong with my ears." I tapped the side of my head with my palm. "Because, see, I thought I heard you say the word 'spider.' And I remember saying 'no insects.'"

Cassie held her hand out to me. And in that hand was a spider. "It's not an insect. Arachnids have eight legs and two body segments. Insects have six legs and three segments."

I swear, I took a look at that spider and almost passed out.

"Since I knew we were doing this today, I decided to do some reading. This is a wolf spider. It has pretty good eyesight. In fact, it has eight eyes."

Cassie said this like having eight eyes was a good thing. Like eight eyes was something everyone should want.

"Go away, Cassie. Go away. Go away, go away, I am *not* going to morph a spider! *You* can morph a spider. I don't like spiders."

Jake gave me a look. "Marco, Cassie always gets stuck doing the new morphs. Besides, this is more *your* mission than anyone else's."

"What? Why?" I demanded angrily. "Why is this my mission more than yours or Rachel's?"

Jake shrugged. "Erek is your friend."

"My friend? When did I ever say he was my friend? He's not my friend. I barely know the guy!"

"Marco, you're such a wuss," Rachel said.

"Hey, *you* want to be a spider?"

Rachel shuddered slightly. "Sure." She was lying. I just knew it. "If I draw the short straw, I'd love to go spider."

Then she grinned. She couldn't keep a straight face.

"Look, you don't *have* to do this," Jake said. "It's just that we're going to be infiltrating a meeting of The Sharing. The Yeerks are totally on alert for animal morphs. We have to fit into the environment of the lake. Whatever morphs we use have to belong there. We can't be showing up there as lions and tigers and bears."

"Oh, my," Cassie interjected.

"We need good vision, but not standard mammal-type eyes. And we can't all go in the same way. I want two people to hang back as a rescue squad in case we get into a mess. Ax has to go because we need him to see if he can figure out what Erek is. Ax is going in as a spider, and we need someone to go with him."

"Has anyone told Ax about this?"

"He was here earlier. While you were sleeping in late. He said he thought a spider's body was much more sensible than a human's body,"

Cassie said. "His exact words were, 'Ah, good. With eight legs it won't fall over like a human.'"

"Be glad we waited for you at all," Rachel growled. "Just draw a straw."

Jake had five pieces of hay in his fist. There was no way to tell which was the shortest one.

"Hah. I know how to beat this," I said. "It's mathematical. If I choose first, my odds are just one in five. The next person to choose has odds of one in four, then one in three, and so on. So the safest thing to do is choose first."

I took a deep breath, reached out, and yanked up a straw.

I took another deep breath and looked at the very short straw. "Really, it made perfect sense mathematically," I said.

I felt like crying.

Rachel rolled her eyes. "You know, if you're going to be a big baby, I'll do it."

I should have just said "okay." That's what I should have said. What I *did* say to Rachel was, "Don't condescend to me, oh mighty *Xena.* Just because I'm not a reckless idiot doesn't mean I'm a wuss. I've never chickened out on a morph yet. And if Ax is in, so am I. You can hang around and be the backup, Rachel. I'm going where the action is."

To which Rachel replied with a very calm, "Okay."

See, this is why guys and girls should not be in combat together. Because it's much harder for a guy to be a coward when some girl is watching. Especially when she's all gung ho. If it had just been Jake and Tobias, I'd have been weeping and groveling on the ground.

Cassie held out the spider. "It's not bad," she said. "I morphed the spider yesterday, just to see what it was like. *Charlotte's Web* was one of my favorite books."

"It would be," I muttered. Well, that was the clincher. Rachel was ready to go, and Cassie had already done it.

I reached out a finger to touch the spider. It was shaking. My finger, not the spider.

I touched the spider's back. It tried to get away but Cassie closed her hand around the spider and the tip of my finger.

The spider became very still as I acquired it. Thanks to the Andalite technology that had transformed me, the spider DNA entered my system.

Maybe the Yeerks were right. Maybe the Andalites were just the big meddlers of the universe. I know one thing: At that moment, as I touched the spider's bristly body, I really wished the Andalites had found someone else to give this power to.

CHAPTER 9

The lake is in the mountains. It's a long way from where any of us live. And if we'd had to walk it would have taken several days. Fortunately, we didn't have to walk.

We have our own little airline. TWA: Travel With Animorphs.

It was a beautiful day. Just a few puffy clouds in a blue sky. Bright sun. A canopy of trees spread out beneath us as we flew toward the mountains.

With my osprey wings spread wide and the sun toasting the ground so it sent up elevators of warm air, it was as perfect as life can get.

If you overlooked the fact that we were heading toward utter, unspeakable grossness and certain destruction.

<Time to split up,> Tobias said. <The lake is just over that next ridge.>

We had not been flying close together because that would have looked massively suspicious. Two ospreys, a harrier, a bald eagle, a peregrine, and a red-tailed hawk, all flying together? Not in the natural world. But we were all within a mile of each other, and all heading in the same direction.

Tobias went into a lazy upward spiral, hanging back. Rachel and Cassie split off, too. The Yeerks would have heavy security around the meeting of The Sharing. The Yeerks know all about morphing. They would be on alert.

Ax, in a harrier morph, Jake, in his peregrine falcon morph, and I flew on toward the lake, though still far apart.

<You know, one of your kind tried to kill me the other day,> I said to Jake.

<Tobias told me,> Jake said. <Gotta watch out. Falcons rule.>

<Yeah, well I noticed he didn't try it a second time.>

<Don't diss falcons,> Jake said.

<One-on-one in a fair fight, an osprey would kick your butt.>

<As if,> Jake sneered.

<Excuse me,> Ax interrupted. <Is there some special meaning to this conversation that I don't understand?>

<Yeah,> I said. <The meaning is that Jake and I are scared, so we're babbling in a desperate effort not to think about it.>

<Ah. I am frightened, too. I don't really like morphing tiny animals. I keep thinking about all the rest of my mass.>

<Your what?> I asked, not really caring. I was focused on the morphing ahead.

<My mass. When you morph something smaller than yourself, your body mass must go somewhere. So it goes into Zero-space. Zero-space is the space that ships travel through when they are going faster than light. It's not very likely to happen, but sometimes a ship traveling in Z-space will intersect with a temporarily parked mass.>

This got my total, complete attention.

<Wait a minute. Are you telling me that when we get small, all the leftover . . . stuff . . . all the extra flesh and guts and bones go bulging into Zero-space like some big balloon of human tissue?>

<Of course. Where did you think all the mass went?>

I shuddered. <I really didn't think about it.>

Jake was no more thrilled than I was. <So right now there's a big bag of Jake floating in Zero-space? And it's possible some spaceship will zoom along and hit it and splatter it all over?>

<No, no, of course not,> Ax said.

I breathed a huge sigh of relief. Too soon, it turned out.

<Of course no ship would actually *hit* a floating mass,> Ax said, talking to us like we were nitwits. <The ship's shielding systems would disintegrate the mass. That's what troubles me about doing small morphs. It very seldom happens. The odds are millions to one. But it *could* happen.>

Jake and I thought about this for a while. About a spaceship "disintegrating" some big wad of our mass. It was not a pretty picture.

<Hey, Ax?> Jake said. <You know how we wanted you to be honest with us? To tell us everything you know?>

<Yes, Prince Jake.>

<Small change. In the future, don't tell us things that will scare us silly just as we're going into possible battle.>

<A big wad of Marco in Zero-space,> I muttered. <Like hanging your butt out of a car window, waiting for a truck to come along and sideswipe it off.>

Just at that moment, I topped the crest of the ridge. Tall pines nearly scraped my belly. And there, spread out before me, sparkling in the sun, was a large lake nestled between the surrounding hills and mountains.

<Okay, boys,> Jake said. <This is where I peel off. Just one final word. I know spiders eat bugs, so do not, I repeat, do *not*, eat any flies. I'll have enough to worry about in fly morph.>

<Remind me again,> I said. <Why are we doing this instead of staying home and sleeping in late?>

<We're saving the world,> Jake said.

<Oh, yeah. Great. My mass is hanging out in the Zero-space highway and I'm about to become Spiderman. I knew there had to be a pretty good reason.>

CHAPTER 10

There were probably two hundred people around the lake below us — boys, girls, older people. Some were swimming. Some were water-skiing. Some were grilling burgers and hot dogs over charcoal fires. A lot were just milling around and talking and laughing.

You'd swear it was some kind of big community picnic. From the air they all looked so normal. And probably most of the people below us were normal. But a lot of them were Controllers. And one of them was Erek, who was certainly not normal.

We stayed well back from the lakeshore and dropped down into the trees. We came to rest on the ground, inside a cluster of tall bushes.

My osprey vision and osprey hearing had revealed no one within a hundred yards. But I was tingling with nervousness, just the same.

<Shall we demorph?> Ax asked.

<Not yet. Tobias said he would swing back over, once we were on the ground.>

So we waited there, looking a bit weird, two birds of prey just hanging out inside a bunch of bushes at the edge of the forest. I could hear the whine of power boats out on the water, and closer, little snatches of human laughter.

<Okay, guys.> Tobias's thought-speak voice suddenly spoke in my head. <Looks clear to me. You've got a guy and a girl maybe a hundred yards off. But I think they're making out, so they should be busy for a while.>

I quickly began to demorph. One of the limitations on morphing is that you can't just morph straight from one form to another. You always have to return to your own body in between.

In Ax's case this meant returning to his Andalite form. That had to make him nervous. There were dozens of Controllers just a few hundred feet away. Yeerks might overlook one kid sneaking around. They wouldn't overlook an Andalite.

<Are you ready to morph again?> Ax asked me, once we were back in our normal bodies.

"I'll *never* be ready to morph a spider," I said. My teeth were chattering, and it wasn't cold.

<I have to morph,> Ax said. <I can't stay here in Andalite form.>

"Yeah, yeah, I know. I know. Okay. Okay, I'm going to do this. But I'm going to keep my eyes closed."

I focused my mind on the spider. But I lost concentration, mostly because even the image of that wolf spider grossed me out. Then Ax started to change. I knew *I* couldn't just stand there and watch. I knew I had to morph.

"It can't be any worse than morphing a fly, right? Or an ant?" I asked no one. Not that I wanted to think about the ant morph. We'd had a very, very, *very* bad time in ant morph.

I closed my eyes and focused again. This time I kept my concentration.

I felt myself starting to shrink. Shrinking is always a little weird, but now I was also thinking about some big, disgusting balloon of Marco mass suddenly bulging out into Zero-space.

Whatever Zero-space was.

I could feel myself getting smaller. I could feel very strange things happening inside me: sudden feelings of emptiness where organs were simply disappearing.

And there was a distracting squishy sound that came up my spine and through my skull.

65

The sound of bones turning to marrow, and of marrow sort of oozing away.

I wouldn't be needing any bones, I guess.

I kept my eyes tightly shut, not wanting to see what was happening. And I held on to my fears with a death grip of determination. I mean, if there's anything worse than being a spider, it's being some disgusting mix of half human, half spider.

But then . . .

POP! POP! POP!

I could see! I tried to close my eyes, but no! I didn't have eyelids. It's very hard to close your eyes when you don't have eyelids.

Eyes were popping open in my forehead. Eyes were erupting out of my head like zits.

I almost lost it right then. I would have screamed if I'd had a voice any longer. But I was already half spider. And I was staring at Ax as he underwent a change very similar to my own.

I was watching him with vision that was half human and half the shattered, broken-mirror vision of the spider's compound eyes.

Something horrifying was growing from the place on Ax's face where a mouth should have been. Something huge and bulging and foul. Two monstrous, swollen things like . . . like nothing I'd ever seen before. They were jaws, but huge and outsized. From the end of each one, a wicked, curved fang grew.

Sometimes you really, really need eyelids. There are definitely some things you don't want to have to see.

I knew the same thing was happening to me. My bulging jaw parts grew till they entered my own distorted field of vision.

Fortunately, I didn't have to worry too long about the jaws. See, I became distracted when legs suddenly exploded from my chest.

SPROOOT!

Four new legs, two on each side, just shot out of me, like I was a tube of toothpaste someone had stomped. They sprouted all Gumby-unformed, then began to form joints. Way too many joints.

My human legs and arms were changing to match these first spider legs. I fell forward, no longer able to stand erect.

It wasn't much of a fall. I was already pretty small. The pine needles beneath me already seemed to be as big around as a human finger.

Not that I had any fingers left to compare with.

All the while, new eyes kept opening suddenly where eyes absolutely did not belong. Some were compound eyes. Some weren't.

Then, as if the extra legs, and the mix 'n'

match eyes, and the huge jaw-and-fang combo weren't enough, some new leglike things came sprouting out of my . . . well, out of where my neck used to be. They were like extra legs, only they weren't. I had no idea what they were. But they moved. Much later, I found out they're called *pedipalps.* A sort of cross between a mouth part and a leg.

My head was swelling, compared to the rest of my body. It was gigantic . . . in a small way. My entire body was now divided into two big chunks: a sort of bulging head and an even bulgier body.

I was almost entirely spider now. The pine needles that had seemed as big as fingers were now as big as two-by-fours.

As the last touch, strangely soft hairs began to grow from everywhere on my body.

It was the hair that seemed to trigger the awakening of the spider brain.

The wolf spider has good eyes for a spider. But it's all the thousands of tiny hairs that really get the spider brain's attention. They sense every subtle clue in the wind. Every minor movement in every direction.

And all of a sudden it felt like the whole world was moving: leaves, pine needles, the dirt beneath my claw-tipped eight legs, bugs in the dirt, moles under the ground, birds in the air.

All of it seemed to be hardwired into the hairs that covered my spider body.

With all that sensory overload, the spider brain woke up. I had been afraid it would be like the brain of an ant: a mindless machine. Or that it would be the terrified, fearful, panic-stricken mind of a prey animal.

But oh, no. Definitely no.

They didn't call it a wolf spider for nothing.

This guy was tiny, no more than two inches from the end of one outstretched leg to the end of the farthest back leg. A toddler could easily crush him underfoot.

But I guess it isn't size alone that makes a predator, because as soon as I felt the edge of that spider brain I knew this boy was trouble.

The wolf spider was a killer.

CHAPTER 11

Hunger.

That was pretty much what the spider mind had to say: hunger. It was hungry. It wanted to hunt. It wanted to kill. It wanted to eat up a few nice juicy bugs. It was hungry.

Did I mention hunger?

And it didn't care what kind of bug. Could be beetles, could be grasshoppers, could be crickets, could be a big mean mantis. The spider didn't care. It ruled the world of bugs. It was to bugs what a lion is to a herd of antelopes. It was a shark among guppies.

They could run from the wolf spider, but they couldn't hide.

Motion! Something moved, left to right across

my field of vision, and I was after it like a dog after a rabbit.

Eight legs powered up and I blew across the forest floor like a drag racer firing out of the starting gate.

The world was weird to my eight spider eyes. I saw colors no human ever saw. It was like when you mess with the color and tint knobs on the TV. Things that should have been brown were blue, and green was red, or whatever. From some angles the pictures were almost clear, but a second later everything would shatter into bits and I'd be watching a million tiny monitors at once.

I never could make logical sense out of it.

But mostly what I saw was movement. I was very, very interested in movement. My eyes and every hair on my disgusting little body were about spotting movement.

And when the right thing moved, my body just answered all on its own.

It was a rush, as they used to say in my dad's day. A charge. It was like tapping into the main pipe of adrenaline. It was electric. It was nuclear. I blew across pine needles and fallen leaves and over patches of dirt and I kept that moving bug in my field of vision and I knew what I was doing, I mean, I knew I was Marco, a human in morph, and I knew I didn't really want to eat that racing bug, but man, I was too jazzed to stop.

The prey was running and I was the predator. I had evolved for hundreds of millions of years to do exactly this. When Tyrannosaurus rex was still millions of years away from even thinking about evolving, tiny arachnid hunters were killing and eating. The entire history of Homo sapiens from caveman to soccer mom was a blip in the history of spiders.

I was death on eight legs.

It was a beetle. That's what I was chasing. A big old beetle, much larger than I was. Larger and slower. He grew in my distorted field of vision. He grew and grew and I powered on.

I wish I could explain why I kept on with the hunt. Sometimes the animal brain takes over for a while and sort of overwhelms the human mind. But that's not what was happening to me. I wasn't overwhelmed. I was just into it.

A last burst of speed!

My front legs touched the beetle. He dodged left, but too slow.

I clambered right up on his back.

I positioned my jaws with their deadly fangs, and —

<Marco. What are you doing?>

It was Ax. I scampered down off the beetle, feeling like I'd been caught doing something wrong. The beetle ran on, relieved to have escaped. If beetles can feel relief.

<Nothing. I was just letting the spider be a spider.> It was a pretty good answer, I thought. <I guess its instincts kind of carried me away.>

<Marco, I morphed the identical spider,> Ax said.

I felt a wave of guilt and shame suddenly swell up inside me. <Ax, it was just a cockroach. Who cares? Come on, we have a job to do.>

<Sometimes humans worry me,> Ax said.

I didn't ask him what he meant. Why had I gotten so into the hunt? Why hadn't I resisted the urge?

I flashed on the rage I'd felt when I talked to Tom. Was that it?

<I think it's this way,> Ax said. He took the lead and I saw him moving in front of me, a spider scurrying effortlessly on his eight legs.

I fell in behind him. I was calm now. The incredible, insane rush of the chase was over. Now the spider was just a tool I was using.

Suddenly, from the sky . . . something fell toward me!

It landed right between Ax and me. A grasshopper, three, four times our size. It looked like an elephant.

Then . . . thwap! It fired its huge hind legs and shot into the air. It disappeared as quickly as it had arrived.

We raced on through the forest, covering the

two hundred feet between us and the edge of the party. I sensed the nearness of humans. I "heard" vibrations that might have been speech, but the voices were too garbled to make any sense out of.

<Hey, Marco, Ax, you guys around?>

It was Jake's thought-speak voice.

<Yes, Prince Jake,> Ax answered. <We are here.>

<We're not pretty, but we're here,> I added.

<Cool. I'm not exactly handsome myself. I'm in fly morph. Haven't found our boy Erek yet, though.>

Something massive and slow appeared in the air above me. I scampered sideways. It landed slowly with a loud WHOOOMPHHH!

A human foot. A shoe. Nike.

<You know, I'd been worrying someone might step on me,> I said. <But humans are so slow.>

<Be careful anyway,> Jake said. <Let me know if you find Erek.>

<I don't know how I'm supposed to recognize him,> I complained. <These spider eyes aren't good at seeing distances. And human heads seem to be way up in the clouds, from where I'm crawling down here.>

But Ax and I went on, skittering swiftly through a forest of huge, slow-moving legs and feet.

Then, right in front of me, I saw it.

It looked like a bare human foot. Except that I

could see through the skin. Through the toenails. With my eight strange, distorted spider eyes I could see right through the electronic haze of the hologram.

I could see what was beneath the hologram.

I saw what looked like interlocking plates of steel and ivory. The "foot" had no toes. In fact, it wasn't shaped like a human foot. More like a paw.

It was not human. And everything in my tingling, buzzing, hyper, spider's senses told me it was not alive.

<Ax?>

<Yes, I see it.>

<What is it?>

<I do not know.>

<It looks like a machine, almost. Like it's made out of metal.>

<Yes,> Ax said. <I think your friend Erek may be an android.>

<An android?>

CHAPTER 12

<Yes. A robot. A machine made to seem like a life-form,> Ax said, as though it was just the most common idea in the world.

<This is like something you know about, Ax?> I asked, looking up at the thing called Erek.

<This is not a type of android I know,> Ax said. <It is not Andalite. I don't think it is Yeerk. I don't know who . . . or *what* . . . it is.>

My spider eyes could see the foot and most of the way up the leg. It was like looking at a double-exposure photograph. There was the outward appearance of a human leg and, way up high, shorts. But beneath all that there was this machine made of what seemed like steel and ivory.

It was thousands of interlocked plates, almost like the chain mail armor knights used to wear. Each of the individual links was roughly triangular in shape. The "ivory" segments were a little larger than the segments that looked like steel.

The robot . . . android . . . whatever it was, was smaller than the human Erek. The leg I was looking at was oddly constructed. More like a stretched-out dog leg than a human leg.

The robot leg, along with its holographic projection of a human foot, lifted off, as Erek went on his way.

<Jake?> I called.

<Yeah? Hey, I think I see our guy. There's this person . . . it's hard with fly senses, but I see this person who is kind of shimmering all over, and it's like there's something hiding underneath all the shimmering light.>

<Yep. That's him,> I confirmed.

<Wait a minute! There's another one!>

<*What*?>

<Another one of *them*,> Jake answered. <I just buzzed right past him. There are two of these things.>

<Okay, *now* things have gotten —> I started to say.

77

FWAP! FWAP! FWAP! FWAP!

A hurricane of wind!

The ground in front of me exploded as two big taloned feet landed in the dirt.

A shadow over my head! I ran.

Two big black triangles came down from the sky above me. They dug in, just in front of me! Just behind me!

Like a power shovel, the two triangles closed together. I was inside. I was in darkness. Total darkness. Some big, muscular thing was crushing me, squeezing me.

I couldn't breathe. I couldn't see. I was being squeezed and pummeled.

And then I realized . . .

I was being swallowed.

<AAAAAHHHHH!> I yelled.

There are two kinds of thought-speak. Private, which is like whispering right in one person's ear, and public, which is like yelling.

I was yelling.

Every person near that lake heard me. Normal humans, who probably wondered, "What was that?" And Controllers, who knew it was thought-speak.

But I didn't care. I was being swallowed.

<Marco!> Jake yelled. <What's happening?>

<Marco! Everyone can hear you!> Ax warned.

I tried to control my panic. I was being swallowed, but I wasn't dead yet.

<Something . . . something just grabbed me!> I said, aiming my thought-speak at Jake and Ax only.

<I think it was a bird,> Ax said. <I saw it. Very big and black. It flew off.>

My spider legs were crushed against my side. Two of them were broken. The hairs all over my body were blind. My eyes were blind. There wasn't enough air even for my spider body to live on.

I was being forced down the gullet of a bird, flying through the air, and seconds away from suffocating.

<Tobias?> I cried desperately. <Can you hear me?>

<Marco? What's happening?> Tobias answered. His reply came from far off.

<A bird ate me. Black bird. We're flying. Can you see . . . ? Help!>

<Marco, there are a dozen big crows flying. I can't tell which one.>

I felt my mind beginning to fade. The spider was dying. *What would happen if the spider died?* I wondered, as my attention drifted away. *What would happen to the big wad of Marco mass in Z-space?*

That thought did it. I was outta there.

Morph out!

I tried to form a mental picture of my own real self. A mental picture of a human named Marco. But it was all confused. My mind was dying, and as it sank it called up a thousand images. Images of wolves and giant ants and gorillas. Images of all the animals I had been, all the minds I had lived in.

I couldn't grab that human image and hold onto it. But then, floating up in my disintegrating consciousness, came the image of my mother.

I guess that's not a surprise. They say dying soldiers on the battlefield often call out for their mothers with their dying breaths. And I guess that's what I was doing, too.

But this was my real mother. The way she'd been when she was truly alive. Not the Controller. Not the Controller known as Visser One, but my own real mom.

She was smiling at me. She was much taller than me, but she bent down to pick me up. I flew, up in the air, up to her face. She kissed me.

"You are going to grow up to be so cute," she said. "My little Marco."

Marco. The human boy. I saw myself clearly then, like I was looking through her eyes at the little toddler I'd been. Not the Animorph Marco, but the little kid Marco.

Suddenly . . .

The pressure was growing. Growing. I was squeezed from all sides. I felt muscle tensing to restrain me, but then, the muscle weakened and quivered.

A ripping, tearing sound!

Light! Light!

I was demorphing. Demorphing and growing. I had burst through the throat of the crow! And now, I was falling!

<Marco!> Tobias yelled.

Muddy, distorted vision showed me the crow falling alongside me.

I was falling. Falling through the air, a vile mix of crippled spider and emerging human.

I was the size of a baseball, I guess, and getting bigger. I hate to even think of what I looked like. I know I wasn't pretty.

WHAMMMMM!

I hit the ground. I bounced. I hit the ground again.

I lay there, not knowing where I was, or what I was. But I knew one thing for sure. I was going to demorph. I was getting OUT OF THAT MORPH!

If I'd had a mouth, I would have started screaming and never stopped. But my mouth reappeared late. Four of my spider legs withered and disappeared. My remaining legs became human arms and legs. My tiny claws became toes. My fangs and jaws became teeth and lips.

81

My eight spider eyes shut down one after another, leaving only two. And slowly, those two eyes became fully human.

I looked up through human eyes at a blue sky. At the high branches of trees looming above me.

And then, I looked up into the face of my former schoolmate, Erek.

Erek the android.

CHAPTER 13

"Marco?" Erek said. "Didn't you used to have longer hair?"

The hair thing again. Anyway, to my human eyes Erek looked completely, one hundred percent human. I knew it wasn't true, but even so, it was almost impossible not to believe the holographic projection that surrounded the android.

Could I remorph into something powerful enough to . . . to make sure he wouldn't be a problem? Probably not. There were Controllers all around the area. All he had to do was yell for help.

Just then, a girl came running up. She looked down at me, then at Erek.

"Who is this?" the girl asked.

83

"His name is Marco," Erek said calmly. "You know the 'Andalite bandits' Chapman is always talking about? The ones who use Andalite morphing technology to carry on a guerrilla war?"

"Of course," she said.

Erek pointed down at me. "I think this human is one of them."

There it was: the end. The end of our existence as Animorphs. We'd always known that if the Yeerks ever discovered our true identities, or even that we were humans, they would wipe us out within a matter of days.

I felt sick. Sick with fear for myself, and for the others. I'd blown it. I'd given away our great secret.

Erek jerked his head toward the girl. "This is my friend Jenny."

I was not pleased to meet her.

I heard the sound of people rushing through bushes.

"Nothing over here," Erek said loudly. "Jenny hurt her ankle. I'll help her. Keep searching. I think I heard something over there."

Erek must have noticed the extremely shocked and puzzled expression on my face. He grinned. "'There are more things in heaven and Earth than are dreamt of in your philosophy, Horatio.'"

"Shakespeare?" I said, amazed.

"Yes. *Hamlet.* I saw the very first performance."

"But . . . but that would have been like centuries ago."

Erek nodded. "Do you know where I live?"

I nodded, with my head still down in the dirt.

"Morph into something small enough to escape from here," Erek suggested. "Come to see me at my house, you and your friends. We have a lot to talk about."

For some stupid reason I said, "You're not human. We know you're an android."

"And you're not an Andalite bandit," Erek said.

"How do I know I can trust you?"

Erek shrugged. "I could turn you in, right now. I'd be Visser Three's new best friend. Even the Visser knows how to reward those who carry out his orders well."

"Maybe you want to catch all of us at once," I said. Don't ask me why I was arguing with him. Maybe it was the humiliating position I was in. Maybe I felt like I had to act tough since I was on my back in the dirt, wearing severely unattractive clothing.

Erek squatted down. "Marco, if I gave you to Visser Three, he would get the names of all your friends from you. I know you're a brave person. You'd have to be, to do all you and your friends have done. But you are not brave enough to survive the Visser's torture. You would tell."

I took a couple of seconds to think about that. He was right, of course. I had a healthy respect for the kind of torture Visser Three could inflict.

"We'll be there," I said. "I guess we don't have a choice. You have us by the . . . you have us cold."

Erek shook his head. "It's not like that. It will be a meeting of allies, Marco. You see, we, too, fight the Yeerks."

CHAPTER 14

My dad made chicken for dinner that night. I'd spent the afternoon with my friends, debating the mess with Erek. We'd gone round and round, but in the end we knew we would show up for the meeting. We had no choice, really.

Barbecued chicken, skin-on mashed potatoes, roasted corn on the cob. This was the absolute height of my father's cooking ability. So I had to eat it. I had to.

But man, there is something about popping out through the throat of a bird that totally destroys your appetite for dead bird.

"How is it?" my dad asked.

"Great," I answered.

We were on the deck in our backyard. It was a

house like the house we'd lived in long ago when we were a complete family. After my mom's "death" — that's still how I thought about it — my dad had spiraled down for a long time. He'd lost his job. We'd moved out of the house and ended up living in a pretty terrible apartment on the edge of a bad part of town.

It was okay, really. I mean, having a lot of stuff and a nice house is cool, but it wasn't being poor that bothered me. It was being alone. My father had been off in some world of his own for a long time. I'd been the one who had to cook and clean and all that.

It was nice to have a house and a yard and a barbecue again. But it wasn't about the house. It was that my dad was my dad again.

I know that sounds corny, coming from me.

"Another piece?"

"Sure. Breast." I held out my plate and tried not to think about exploding crows, or the fact that I'd come very close to having beetle for lunch. Sometimes my life was just too weird.

I had questions to ask my father, but I wanted them to sound natural. You know, like I was just making normal conversation.

"So, Dad. What are you doing at work lately?"

He shrugged and gave me a wink. "We're finishing up the observatory project. I still can't figure out what happened there. That software your

‹Never Surrender›

ANIMORPHS

◆ SCHOLASTIC

TM

‹You're Out of Time›

ANIMORPHS

◆ SCHOLASTIC

TM

friend No accidentally created just sort of disappeared."

My friend "No" was really Ax. There was a long story behind all that. You could probably ask our friendly neighborhood Andalite about it, but it wasn't a story I could tell my father.

"What'll you do then, after you get done at the observatory?" I asked, trying to seem totally casual by chomping on corn the whole time.

My dad's eyes flickered toward me, almost suspiciously. He shrugged. "A project I can't talk about for this company called Matcom."

I laughed, trying to stay very casual. "Building a better bomb?"

He didn't answer for a few seconds. Then, in a strange voice, he said, "I've never done weapons research."

I was actually surprised. "Why not?"

"You gonna eat that chicken or just tease it?" He gave me a long look, like he was trying to decide if I was old enough to hear what he was going to say.

I picked up the chicken breast. Chicken wasn't crow, after all.

"It was your mom," he said.

I stopped eating.

"The last year, year and a half before . . . you know. Before. It was like this perfect time for us." He smiled at some picture only he could see. "We used to fight every now and then when you were younger, like most couples. But then it was as if all our problems were gone, settled. Maybe I had changed. Maybe she had. I don't know."

I felt cold fingers around my heart.

"It was the best time of my life," he said. "It was like we'd achieved some level of perfect peace and perfect love. But at the same time, there were these times when your mom would seem upset. Like she was struggling with some problem she wouldn't tell me about."

I had stopped breathing. I knew. I knew now when the change had been made. The perfect love my father was talking about was the Yeerk at work in my mother's head. The Yeerk wasn't interested in stupid little domestic battles. It wanted peace so that it could focus on deeper goals.

"Anyway, one day I woke up in the middle of the night. Your mom was sitting up in bed, wide awake. I knew she'd had a bad dream or something. But it made the hair on the back of my neck stand up. It was just . . ." He shook his head. "It was so strange. She sounded like she was trapped in a deep well, and trying to call out to me."

There were tears in my eyes. I hoped my father wouldn't notice.

"She said, 'They won't take you if you stay away from the military.' It didn't make any sense. But the way she said it . . . like it was the hardest thing she'd ever said . . . like it was the most important thing she'd ever said."

I had some idea just how hard it had been for my mother to say that. Sometimes, when there is some terrible need, the human being crushed beneath the Yeerk can force its way out. It can seize control for a few desperate seconds.

They say the price the human host pays is terrible. The Yeerk has mental tortures it can carry on for weeks.

My mother, my *real* mother, had struck when the Yeerk was distracted, and for a few seconds regained control.

"Anyway," my dad said, "I know it was just your mom having a bad dream. But ever since then, whenever an opportunity came up to do defense work, I just got this bad feeling about it."

I couldn't even pretend to eat any more.

"Dad, are you thinking about taking on a military project now?"

He avoided my gaze. "There are some very exciting things going on with this Matcom. The thing they want me on isn't military in any way. But . . . well, they do carry on some very secret work. I guess some of what they do is probably military."

91

There it was. The reason Tom was trying to get me to bring my father to The Sharing. My father was working on some project that the Yeerks wanted to control.

My mother had warned him. It may have been the last words that she, the real, human woman, ever spoke to him.

He was going to ignore that warning, and now the Yeerks wanted him.

CHAPTER 15

We had decided to meet with Erek at his house. We had not decided to trust him completely.

Jake, Cassie, Ax, and I were going to the meeting.

Rachel and Tobias stayed outside as backup. Rachel was all primed to use her grizzly bear morph if we called for help.

"I'll be within range of Ax's thought-speak," she said for the tenth time. "I can morph my bear in a minute and go through that door about ten seconds later."

"If you do that, try not to stomp over me in the process, okay?" I said.

I glanced up and saw Tobias swooping down to settle in the tree in Erek's yard.

I could joke about it, but the truth was, it did feel reassuring to know Rachel and Tobias were ready to be the cavalry.

We went up to the front door of the very ordinary-looking house. I sent Jake a look that said, "Man, I hope we're right about this." But Jake was busy exchanging solemn glances with Cassie.

"So? Someone knock on the door," I said. I glanced at Ax. He was in his human morph. His human morph is made up of DNA gathered at the same time from all of us except Tobias. There's some of Jake and Rachel and Cassie and me in Ax's human shape. In the end result he's male, but almost as pretty as a girl.

Plus, he's annoying in human morph.

"Knock? Knock on the door? Why? Knockon. Knock-kuh."

Andalites don't have mouths, and Ax can't get over how fun it is to make actual sounds. Plus, you don't even want the boy in the same room with certain foods.

Jake knocked.

The door opened. I was surprised. It wasn't Erek. It was his father, Mr. King.

He nodded. "Come in."

We stepped inside. I felt completely dorky. It

94

was like we were coming over to ask if Erek could come out and play. I mean, the house looked so normal inside. Normal furniture and normal lights and normal dishes displayed in a hutch. A normal TV on "mute," showing pictures from CNN.

There were two dogs, a Labrador mix and a fat little terrier. The Lab just lolled over on its back. The terrier came running over to sniff our shoes.

"Is Erek here?" I asked.

Mr. King nodded. "Yes. Would you like a soda or anything?"

"No thanks, Mr. King," Cassie said. She bent over to scratch behind the terrier's ears.

"You like dogs?" Mr. King asked.

"She likes any animal," I answered. "She even likes skunks."

"But dogs, do you like dogs?"

Cassie smiled. "If reincarnation were real, I'd want to come back as a dog."

Mr. King smiled, nodding as if Cassie had just said something profound. "Would you all come with me?"

He turned and led the way toward the kitchen. Once again, the total normalcy of it seemed jarring. There were little Post-It notes on the refrigerator saying things like "dozen eggs, bell peppers." Someone had left a box of Wheaties out on the counter.

Mr. King opened a door. It led down to the basement. We followed him down the narrow wooden steps.

At this point I started to wonder. I noticed that Ax was morphing slowly out of his human shape, returning to Andalite form a little at a time.

Good old Ax. He sensed danger and he wanted his tail available.

I wanted his tail available, too.

Mr. King paused when we all got down to the basement. He watched with absolutely no surprise as Ax finished transforming. He waited politely for Ax to be done.

Then, to my utter amazement, I felt a slight dropping sensation. It took a few seconds to realize what was happening. The basement was dropping like an elevator. When I looked up I couldn't see a roof overhead, just darkness.

"Whoa," Cassie commented.

"Don't be afraid," Mr. King said.

It didn't last long. We may have dropped four or five floors. At least that's what it felt like to me. Then, with a slight lurch, the basement/elevator stopped.

"Is this the floor for men's clothing?" I asked.

I was almost not surprised when one entire wall of the basement, hung with tools and garden hose and a rake and hoe, simply disappeared.

Where the wall had been was now a hallway lit with a golden light.

"My basement won't do this," I muttered to Jake.

"Have you ever tried?" he asked.

"This way," Mr. King said.

We followed him. It was way too late to start worrying now.

The hallway wasn't long, just fifty feet or so. It reached a dead end, a blank wall. But then that wall, too, disappeared.

"Yah!"

"No way!"

<Strange.>

"This is just a hologram, right?" I said. But somehow, I knew it wasn't. It was real. Unbelievable, yet real.

What was beyond the hallway was a vast, vast chamber, lit in glowing gold light, soft and buttery warm.

I stepped out of the hallway onto springy grass. And over my head, maybe a hundred feet up, there was a glowing orb, like a sun. That's where the yellow light came from.

Stretched out before us, for more than the length of a football field, was a sort of park. Trees, grass, streams, flowers, butterflies flying around jerkily, bees buzzing from flower to flower, squirrels racing up and down the trees.

Walking here and there were androids. Androids in their natural form, machines made of steel and something white. The androids had mouths that were almost like muzzles, clumsy-looking legs, and stubby fingers.

But it wasn't the presence of half-dozen or so androids that was really shocking. What was really shocking was that there were hundreds, maybe even a thousand dogs. Normal, everyday Earth dogs, every breed and half-breed you could imagine, running in packs, yipping, yapping, bowwowing, howling, growling, ruff-ruffing dogs. They were chasing squirrels, smelling each other, and generally having a great ole dog time.

Jake, Cassie, and I stood there with our jaws hanging open like complete idiots. If Ax had possessed a mouth, his would have been hanging open, too.

It was doggie heaven. Dogs and robots in a huge, underground park.

One of the robots came trotting toward us. As it got near, a hologram shimmered around it. A second later, it was Erek.

"Welcome," he said. "I guess you're probably a little surprised."

CHAPTER 16

"We are the Chee," Erek said.

Mr. King had left, and Erek had brought us to a place beneath a large tree. A little stream trickled by, just a few feet away. A wall of silence had come down, as if someone had turned down the sound of all the barking dogs. I could still hear them, but it was as if the sound were far away now.

<You are androids,> Ax commented.

"Yes."

<You show a very high level of technological sophistication,> Ax said.

Erek smiled with what looked exactly like human lips. "We are just the creation. It is our creators who were the great builders."

99

"Why did you bring us down here?" Jake asked. "Why show us all this?"

"We want you to trust us," Erek said. "We know that you're suspicious. You have to be. I'm sure you've left some of your people outside, just in case we betray you. I wanted us to be equal. I wanted you to know our secrets, since we know yours."

"We saw you at the concert," I started to say.

He looked surprised, then nodded. "Ah, yes. You were the two dogs, weren't you? I sensed something odd about you. Tell me: What's it like to actually be a dog?"

"It's truly cool," Jake said. "You knew we were the two dogs?"

Erek shook his head. "We didn't know, but I felt something strange. We've known there were morph-capable forces on Earth. There is very little that the Yeerks know that we don't also know."

"You were handing out flyers for The Sharing. You were at a meeting of The Sharing," I accused.

"True. But maybe I should tell you our story. Then you'll understand who we are. And why we are your allies. And also why we . . . or at least *some* of us . . . would like your help."

"That would be nice," Cassie said.

You have to say one thing for Erek: The boy

knew how to tell a story. Suddenly, everything around us dissolved. In its place there grew a vast, three-dimensional picture. It looked as real as Erek.

We were no longer on Earth. There were two suns in the sky, one small and almost red, the other four times as big as Earth's sun and a deeper gold.

The trees and flowers and grasses around us were definitely not anything that had ever grown on Earth. The trunks of the trees were green and smooth. But instead of leaves, the branches just kept splitting into ever smaller branches and twigs that grew gradually from green to silver to a brilliant shade of pink. These pink twigs were all intertwined, so that from a distance the trees looked like huge balls of pink steel wool.

The trees were no larger than Earth trees, it seemed to me, but what was huge were the mushrooms. At least, they looked kind of like mushrooms. They were half as large as the trees themselves. Messy nests of some leathery, leaping, three-legged animal seemed to be perched on each of the mushrooms.

There were other animals around, each stranger than the last. But the main animal we saw was a two-legged creature that stood maybe four feet tall. It had long, floppy ears and a muzzle.

It looked weirdly like a dog that could walk on its hind legs. It looked, in fact, a little like Erek when he dropped the hologram and showed his true self.

"Our creators," Erek said. "They were known as Pemalites. A hundred thousand years before the Andalites learned to make fire, the Pemalites were capable of faster-than-light travel."

I noticed Ax's tail twitch a little at that.

"And of course, humans were just hairy apes when the Pemalites first visited Earth. The Pemalites were not interested in conquest, or in interfering in the lives of other planets. They enjoyed life." Erek smiled. "They loved to play. They loved games and jokes and laughter. And they had been a fully evolved race for so long that all the harsher instincts were gone from them. They had no evil in their hearts. They had no evil in their souls."

I found this hard to believe. But as I watched the hologram around me, it was possible to believe that on this weird planet the Pemalites had found some deep inner peace. There was just a sense of deep calm about the place. Like one of those Zen gardens or something. It just felt peaceful. Peaceful, but not dead or tired or boring. In fact, everywhere I looked, I saw Pemalites jumping around, chasing, playing, and making an odd CHUK CHUK CHUK that must have been laughter.

The scene around me changed, like a movie doing a flash-forward. Now, mingled in with the Pemalites, were androids like Erek. The androids looked vaguely like their canine creators.

"We were toys, originally," Erek said. "The Pemalites made us to play with. They called us the Chee. It's a word that means 'friend.' They also had work for us to do, but they created us mostly to be their companions. An artificial race, yes, but not a race of mechanical slaves."

Erek looked at us and I swear there were tears in his holographic eyes. "We were their friends and equals and companions. They taught us to laugh and play. They loved it when they were able to create androids who could tell a joke. There was a celebration that lasted a year."

Then . . . ZZZZZZZAAAAAAAARRRRPPPP!

I jerked back. A monstrous beam of light sliced the ground open right in front of us, like some insane plow tearing up the earth. It incinerated the pink Brillo pad trees and the huge mushrooms.

"Then the Howlers came," Erek explained. "They suddenly popped out of Zero-space, thousands of powerful ships. They had come from clear outside this galaxy. The Pemalites had no idea who they were. And they never found out what the Howlers wanted. The Howlers made no demands. They just attacked. Maybe that's all they wanted: to destroy."

What Erek showed us next was like one of those horrifying films from World War II. Pemalites hunted from the air. Pemalite space stations blown apart. Pemalite ships sliced open, and helpless Pemalites left to drift through cold, dead space. The scenes of massacre just went on and on.

I noticed Cassie was crying. I think I was crying, too. It was too horrible.

"Almost the entire race of Pemalites was wiped out," Erek said. "A few hundred Chee and a few hundred Pemalites left the planet, escaping in a single ship just seconds ahead of a new wave of Howler attacks.

"We escaped into Zero-space. We had no plan, no idea what to do."

"Why didn't you fight back?" I demanded. "I mean, you talk about how advanced the Pemalites were. If they could create androids, they could create weapons."

Erek looked at me and nodded, like he agreed. "The Pemalites had forgotten the ways of conflict and war. They were creatures of peace. They'd forgotten that there could be such a thing as pure evil."

104

That answer just frustrated me. It made no sense. But I let Erek tell the rest of his grim story.

"As we ran for our lives through Zero-space, we discovered that the Howlers had achieved a special revenge. The Pemalites began to become sick. They began to die. The Howlers had unleashed germ weapons. The Pemalites were doomed. But we Chee, we androids, were unaffected."

The scene around us became the inside of a space ship. A scene of Chee, looking on helplessly while one of their creators writhed in pain.

"Then we remembered a planet. A planet similar to our own, but very far from our home and the Howlers. It had only one sun and the light was pale, but there were trees and grass and wonderful oceans."

"Earth," Cassie said.

"Earth," Erek said. "The Pemalites had not visited Earth in fifty thousand years, and in that time, everything had changed. The wandering tribes of primates had created cities. They had domesticated animals. They were planting crops.

"We landed on Earth with just six Pemalites still clinging to life."

The hologram disappeared, and the underground cavern was back to its normal self — a wide park of Earth trees and Earth plants, with dogs everywhere.

"We could not save the Pemalites. They would die. But we could try and rescue some *part* of them. We hoped we could keep their hearts, their souls alive somehow. We looked for an Earth species we could use to harbor the essence of the Pemalites. Their decency. Their kindness. Their playfulness and love."

"Wolves," Cassie said, once again way ahead of me.

Erek looked surprised, but he nodded his holographically projected human head. "Yes. They looked most like the Pemalites themselves. We grafted the essence of the Pemalites into the wolf species. And from that union, dogs were created. To this day, most dogs carry within them the essence of the Pemalites. Not all, but most. Wherever you see a dog playing, chasing a stick, running around barking for the sheer joy of life, you see the remnants of the race of Pemalites."

"That's why all these dogs are here," Jake said. "They're your . . . what, friends? Creators?"

"They are our joy," Erek said, "because they remind us of a world without evil. The world we lost. We Chee are all that is left of Pemalite technological genius. The dogs of Earth are all that is left of Pemalite souls."

106

CHAPTER 17

I don't think I would have believed any of it. Except for the small fact that we were in a huge underground park. And there were androids walking around.

Plus, there was the fact that my entire life had become one long, incredible, unbelievable story. So who was I to laugh at Erek's story?

"So you all pass as humans?" I asked Erek.

He nodded. "Yes. We live as humans. We play the role of children and then grow older, and eventually our hologram is allowed to 'die' and we start again as children."

"How long has this been going on?" Cassie asked.

Erek smiled warmly. "I helped to build the great pyramid."

"You designed the pyramids?"

"No, no, of course not. We have never interfered in human affairs. I was a slave. I helped to quarry the stone. It was a challenge, because I was new at pretending to be human. I had to hide my real strength, of course. The Pemalite home world had a gravity four times stronger than Earth's. Naturally, we were designed for that gravity, which means we are quite powerful by human standards."

"And you stayed as a slave?" Jake asked. "You could have taken over Egypt. You could have taken over the world."

"No. We are not the Yeerks," he said coldly. "You see, when our creators made us, they hardwired us for nonviolence. We are not capable of hurting another living being. No Chee has *ever* taken a life."

Just then, I noticed a group of four Chee walking quickly toward us.

Erek saw them, too. Even though I know his "face" was just a hologram, it seemed to me he was annoyed.

"What have you done?" one of the Chee demanded. "What have you done, you fool?"

The four Chee came up and glared at us with

robot eyes. "Humans? An Andalite? Here? What have you told them?"

"Everything," Erek said defiantly. "These are the ones, these humans and this Andalite, who have been resisting the Yeerks. They're the ones who can morph." His voice rose. "They are the ones who are fighting the battle *we* should fight."

"We are Chee. We do not fight," one of the androids said. It turned on its holographic projector. A human body appeared. The body of an old woman, maybe eighty years old.

"I am Chee-Ionos. My human name for now is Maria," she said. "I did not mean to seem angry toward you humans, or you, my Andalite friend. My dispute is with this Chee called Erek and some of his friends."

"We stood by helplessly as the Howlers annihilated our creators," Erek said to Maria. "We can't stand by helplessly and watch this world be destroyed, too. Dogs and humans are intertwined. They have evolved a dependency. Dogs cannot survive without humans. If the humans fall to the Yeerks, we, the last great masterpieces of the Pemalites, and the dogs, their spirit-homes, will all die, too."

I gave Jake a look. That's why the Chee wanted to help humans? To save dogs? Jake shook his head slightly in amusement.

"We do *not* fight," Maria said heatedly. "We do *not* kill. You know that, Erek. Yet you bring these outsiders here. You blurt the secrets we have kept for thousands of years. Why? What good can come from it? We cannot fight to save the humans."

"That's where you're wrong," Erek said softly. "We *can* fight. While you and the others merely hope everything will work out, my friends and I have been infiltrating the Yeerk organizations here on Earth. The Yeerks even think that I am one of *them*."

Maria and the three unhologrammed Chee just stared.

"The Yeerks have been busy. They control a computer company called Matcom."

It took me a couple of seconds to remember that name.

Erek went on. "The Yeerks are working on a master computer to infiltrate and rewrite all the software in all the computers on Earth. When they have achieved sufficient force among humans, they will launch this computer bomb, and in a flash, control all computers."

"What does this have to do with us?" Maria asked.

"The heart of this system is a crystal the Yeerks obtained from a Dayang trader. The Dayang didn't know what he had. But the Yeerks

110

did. The crystal is a processor more sophisticated than anything even the Andalites could create. And it is more than fifty-thousand Earth years old."

"A Pemalite crystal!" Maria gasped.

"Yes. A Pemalite crystal. If we had it, we could rewrite our own internal systems. Do you understand now? We could erase the prohibition against violence. We could be free! Free to fight!"

"A Pemalite crystal," Maria whispered. "You can't do this, Erek. You can't!"

But Erek just turned away. "If we can get the crystal, there is very little we can't do. Our strength, joined with these Animorphs? The Yeerks would have to double their forces just to contain us."

<How did you convince the Yeerks that you are one of them?> Ax asked him.

Erek turned off his hologram and became a machine once again. And then the front of his head split open. Inside his steel and ivory head was a chamber, just a few inches in diameter.

And inside that chamber was a gray slug, helpless, unable to escape. Tiny wires, no thicker than hairs, wrapped around it.

<Yeerk!> Ax hissed.

"Yes," Erek said. "The Yeerks believe I am human. I accepted infestation. But of course the

111

Yeerk cannot make a Controller of me. I made a place for him instead. He sees nothing. Knows nothing. I tapped *his* memory, not the other way around. And now I can pass among the Yeerks like one of them."

I had two reactions. One, I was sick at the thought of that Yeerk, trapped inside a steel cage. As much as I hated Yeerks, it seemed harsh just the same.

But another reaction was much stronger. We had an ally! A powerful ally. An android who could pass as a Controller, who could enter Yeerk society. And an android with many powers of his own.

"How do you keep the Yeerk alive without Kandrona rays?" Cassie asked.

See, every three days a Yeerk has to return to the Yeerk pool to absorb Kandrona rays. Without that, they die.

"I am able to use my own internal power to generate Kandrona rays to keep this Yeerk alive," Erek explained. "When I go to the Yeerk pool I am able to trick the Yeerks into believing that my Yeerk is swimming in the pool. I generate a hologram of a Yeerk leaving my ear and dropping into the pool. Later, I create a hologram of it returning. The Yeerks never notice that they don't encounter this Yeerk actually *in* the pool. Yeerks communicate very little in their natural states."

"How do we fit into all this?" Jake asked. "I mean, what do you want with us, Erek?"

Erek resumed his human appearance. He stepped toward us, eager, excited. "We could fight together against the Yeerks. We could be allies. If only . . . we need that Pemalite crystal. But the Yeerks have created a maze of defenses like nothing you can imagine. That crystal is in a room at the heart of the Matcom building. There are Hork-Bajir everywhere. Elite Hork-Bajir warriors, the best.

"And the crystal itself is guarded by an ingenious system. It is concealed in a room of absolute darkness. Absolute darkness. The slightest, faintest light, ultraviolet, infrared, any light, will set off alarms. Within the darkness are wires that are set off by the slightest touch."

"So to get to the crystal you'd have to be able to find it without seeing it, and avoid the wires that are also invisible in the darkness," I said.

"It's like finding a needle in a haystack when you're blindfolded and can't touch a single piece of hay. The walls, ceiling, and floor are all pressure-sensitive, so you can't touch them. It may be impossible," Erek said.

"How are we supposed to do that?" I demanded. "How can you find something you can't see? It's not like it'll smell or call out to us."

"Um . . ." Cassie said.

"Excuse me?" Jake asked in surprise.

"It can be done," Cassie said. "I mean . . . if we *want* to."

"Of course we want to," I said. "With these guys on our side, we actually have a chance of winning. Of *course* we want to. Animorphs and Chee together? Our morphing ability, their strength and holographic tricks? We'd kick Yeerk butt."

"No," Maria cried. "You don't understand. Chee do not hurt. Chee do not kill. No Chee has ever taken a life." She grabbed my arm and looked right in my eyes. "While humans and Yeerks and Andalites and Hork-Bajir and a million other species on a million worlds warred and slaughtered and conquered, we remained at peace. Would you end all that? Would you make us killers, too?"

"Yes, ma'am, I guess I would," I said, a little coldly. "We're in a fight for our lives here. Our parents, our brothers and sisters, our friends — they are all going to be slaves of the Yeerks, if we don't win. So I'll do whatever it takes. If you'd fought all those thousands of years ago, the Pemalites would still be alive. And you wouldn't be living with dogs in a big underground kennel."

I didn't mention the sudden interest The Sharing had in my father. I didn't want to make this personal.

Maria let me go, and Erek nodded.

"A big underground kennel," Erek said bitterly. "Exactly."

"We'll get your crystal for you," Jake said. "Tell us all you know about this Matcom, and we'll get your crystal." He looked at the Chee called Maria. "Sorry, but Marco is right. The Yeerks have my brother. There's nothing I won't do to get him back."

CHAPTER 18

We rode the fake basement back up, leaving the eerie golden world of dogs behind.

"So. Do we have a deal?" Erek asked. "You'll help us get the Pemalite crystal? And then we'll fight alongside you to defeat the Yeerks."

"Sounds good to me," I said quickly.

"Unless anyone has any objection —" Jake started to say.

That's when Cassie interrupted. "Erek, let us talk it over. It's a big decision."

I was surprised, but not as surprised as Jake was.

Then we heard a noise coming from directly above us.

"HhhhrrrAAAAWWWWRRRR!"

"Oh, man," I said. I knew that sound. We all knew that sound.

"Rachel," Cassie said under her breath.

"We were down there a long time," Jake said. "Erek, I think a friend of ours may have come in to rescue us."

Erek shrugged. "I don't think it's going to be a problem."

"You don't know our friend," I said.

The basement had settled back into its normal place. I tore up the stairway. "Rachel! Chill!"

I burst back into the utterly normal kitchen and raced into the utterly normal living room.

The front door of the house had been ripped off its hinges. The couch was thrown against one wall. And there, in the middle of the room, standing so tall its head scraped the ceiling, was a full-grown grizzly bear.

"HhhhRRAAAAWWRRR!" Rachel roared in rage and frustration.

Frustration, see, because the Chee who passed as Erek's father had her in a full nelson. His human-holograph arms were wrapped around the unbelievably massive shoulders of the grizzly, and he was actually holding the great bear still.

He had pinned a grizzly so powerful it could literally turn a Toyota into an aluminum can.

"Okay, *now* I've seen everything," I said.

<You Chee are very strong,> Ax commented.

117

This was the understatement of all time.

<Where have you been?!> Rachel demanded. <I waited as long as I could. I figured you were dead or something. And if you don't have a good explanation, you *will* be dead!>

"Oh, we have a story, all right," Cassie said.

Rachel had calmed down and stopped roaring when she saw us. Now the Chee slowly released her, and she began to change back out of morph.

Jake looked embarrassed and started to pull the couch back down. "Um, Erek, this is our friend Rachel."

"It was smart of you to keep a reserve," Erek commented. To Rachel he said, "I hope you weren't hurt."

"How come you can wrestle a grizzly if you have to be nonviolent?" I asked Erek.

"Of course, my 'father' here knew she was not a true bear. And he only held onto her. He did not destroy her. If Rachel had been strong enough to win, my 'father' would have had no choice but to allow himself to be destroyed."

I laughed. "I see why you want to change that."

I expected Erek to agree. Instead, he looked a little sad. "Yes," he said. Just that one word.

We started to leave. I let the others get a few steps ahead of me. I pulled Erek over. "Hey,

Erek. You were at my mom's funeral. I don't think I said thanks at the time."

Erek looked away and bit his lip. "Marco . . . there's something I have to tell you."

"I think I already know. My mother isn't dead. She's a Controller. She's Visser One."

It was Erek's turn to be impressed. "You guys have learned a lot."

I shrugged. "Is that why you were at the funeral? Did you know?"

Erek nodded. "I knew. I might have been able to save her . . . if."

I met his gaze. "Too late to save her," I said. "But payback is going to be very painful for those filthy slugs."

On the way home, we filled Rachel and Tobias in on what had happened. It took a while. We were back at Cassie's barn before we were done.

"I say do it," Rachel said. "That Chee guy held onto me like I was a baby. They're strong. They have technology we don't. They've already penetrated The Sharing. They would double our chances. End of story."

"No, *not* end of story," Cassie said, contradicting her friend. "What right do we have to interfere and destroy the thousands of years of peace this species has had? Didn't you hear Maria? No Chee has ever taken another life. You want them to be saying a thousand years from now that no Chee ever took a life till *we* made them killers?"

I rounded on her, angry. "What I don't want a thousand years from now is for people to be saying, 'Too bad about the humans. They ended up as dead as the Pemalites.'"

"Ax?" Jake asked. "You haven't said much."

Ax was in human morph, of course, since we were in the barn. "As you know, we Andalites are not supposed to interfere in the lives of other species. I am already breaking that law with you. And I am proud to be breaking that law in this case. But the Chee . . . Chee! It makes a funny sound, doesn't it? Chee." He smiled with his human mouth, then grew serious again. "The Chee are a different species. Older than Andalites. I feel . . . badly . . . helping another species to become violent."

Rachel said, "Look, no one likes violence. All right? But we didn't ask for this war with the Yeerks. When the bad guys come after you, when *they* start the violence, they leave you no choice: fight or die."

"Fight or die," I agreed. "And you want proof? Look at the Pemalites. They didn't fight, they died. All gone. No more. Scratch a whole species. Now their 'essence,' whatever that means, is stuck inside dogs, and their robots feed them

120

extra kibble. Yippee. That worked out real well for them. And even that's better off than we'll be if we lose to the Yeerks."

"Law of the jungle," Rachel said. "You eat or you get eaten."

<Maybe so,> Tobias said, speaking up for the first time. <But still, wouldn't it be nice if that wasn't the law?>

"How can you take that attitude?" I demanded. "You're a predator. You know how it is."

<Yes. I know exactly how it is. That doesn't mean I like it. Look, the Pemalites were wiped out, maybe because they didn't fight. Maybe they'd have lost even if they had fought. We'll never know. But the Chee have lived for thousands of years. I know they're androids, but they're a species, too. They've survived without killing. Doesn't something about that make you jealous? Don't you wish we could say the same? Don't you wish Homo sapiens could face the universe and honestly say, "We do not kill? We don't enslave. We don't make war"?>

"I don't make the rules," I said. "I didn't start this war. Humans didn't start this war. Look, I don't want to make this personal, but I know the name Matcom. My dad is involved in some work with them. And the other day Tom . . ." I shot a glance at Jake. "His brother was on me to come to The Sharing and bring my father. The Sharing

121

is targeting my dad, and now we know why. So for me, it's simple: If we take this Pemalite crystal, maybe my dad isn't involved with Matcom anymore. And maybe the Yeerks find someone else to infest."

No one had an answer to that. I knew they wouldn't.

Cassie walked down to the far end of the barn and came back carrying a small cage.

"Total darkness, can't touch walls, floor, or ceiling, and you have to travel through a room strung with sensitive wires you can't even see." She held up the cage. "Meet the animal that can do all that."

It was no larger than a small rat with its leathery wings folded back.

"Cool," I said. "First I'm Spiderman, now I get to be Batman."

CHAPTER 19

I thought for once we'd get a chance to practice with the bat morph. We were planning to go after the Pemalite crystal the next weekend. Plenty of time to plan and prepare.

Yeah, right.

"Marco?" My dad yelled up the stairs to my room, where I was desperately trying to figure out some math homework.

"Yeah?"

"Phone."

"'X' equals point oh-three-nine," I reminded myself so I wouldn't lose my place. I went out into the hall to grab the upstairs phone. "Point oh-three-nine. Yeah, who is it?"

"Hi, Marco. It's me, Erek."

"Oh, hi, Erek, what's up?" I hoped he would remember our phones could be bugged.

"Not much," he said, sounding very convincingly human. "I was just thinking, though, you know that thing we were going to do next weekend? Why don't we just do it tonight instead?"

I knew what the "thing" was. And I knew Erek wasn't calling on a whim. Something had gone wrong. I swallowed my heart, which had jumped up into my throat. "Okay. Maybe I'll call Jake and see if he wants to do it, too."

"That'd be excellent," Erek said. "Later, man."

I hung up the phone and thought seriously about pretending I hadn't gotten the call. I mean, I wanted to do this. It was important, life and death. But it was like something out of *Mission: Impossible*. And without planning or practice, it was beyond impossible.

Plus, I had homework to do.

I picked up the phone and called Jake. Four hours later, with all of our parents asleep in their beds, we met at Cassie's barn. All of us, including Ax. Erek arrived last.

He didn't waste time with small talk. "There's a problem. The Yeerks are putting in a brand new security system on top of the existing systems. I don't think it's active yet, but I can't find out what it is."

<Fine. We can wait a few weeks till you can get the details,> Tobias said.

"The crystal is already so well protected that any new system may put it beyond our grasp for good," Erek said. "And don't forget — the Yeerks are racing to use this crystal to create a computer system so powerful it can take over every computer on Earth. They're not there yet. But the longer we wait . . ."

"Oh, man, this sucks," I said. "No planning? No preparation? Just go in and hope for the best?"

"I'll tell you everything I know," Erek said. "Listen carefully. It's not too complicated."

For a few seconds we sort of teetered on the edge. We weren't sure what to do. Erek wanted us to go in, obviously. But he had his own interests, which might not be the same as ours.

It was the worst possible situation. Any one of our parents could wake up and discover we were not at home. That would mean frantic phone calls back and forth from our folks to our friends' parents, calls to the cops, probably search teams out beating the woods.

"Go or don't go?" Jake asked.

"Go," Rachel said, but with less enthusiasm than usual. A lot less.

"Go," I said. "But personally, I can't blame anyone who wants to sit this one out."

Cassie gave me a dirty look. I guess she took it personally. "I say go," she said. "I don't sit anything out, Marco."

<I'm not in this,> Tobias said. <I'm useless on this mission, so I don't vote.>

<I go where Prince Jake goes,> Ax said.

"Don't call me 'prince,'" Jake said wearily for the thousandth time. "Okay, we go."

Erek immediately began telling us all he knew about Matcom and the security for the Pemalite crystal. After about two minutes I was ready to change my vote.

But by then it was too late. We'd made our decision, and it was as if we were being swept toward a waterfall — like a bunch of canoeists who'd lost their last paddle. We'd survive . . . or not . . . but one thing was sure. We were definitely going over the edge.

CHAPTER 20

E rek was not going with us. But he would be waiting outside Matcom when we came out.

Assuming we came out.

We flew from Cassie's barn to the Matcom building. It was one of those boring-looking, three-story glass and cement buildings you see in industrial parks everywhere. Just a bunch of blue glass rectangles with a big parking lot in back.

In fact, it looked so much like every other boring square building in the industrial park, we had trouble finding it. We flew around, a lost gang of owls, for a good fifteen minutes before Rachel spotted the Matcom sign.

We landed on the roof of the building. Erek

had assured us there were no cameras or guards up there.

"Let's find that pipe," Jake whispered as soon as we were all human again. Or, in Ax's case, Andalite.

"Erek said southwest corner, right?" I said.

"*North*west," Cassie said.

She sounded sure, so I decided to agree. "Yeah, that was it. Which way is northwest?"

Ax laughed in thought-speak, till he realized I was serious. <You can't find directions?> He sounded shocked. Like he'd just discovered we had hidden tail blades. <It's that corner over there.>

The pipe was about three inches in diameter.

"I hope this works," I said. "I don't even know if my Spiderman can make silk."

"Spider*woman*," Cassie said. "Your spider morph is female. Wolf spiders don't make webs, but they do make silk. It should work."

"Easy for you say. I don't even know how to turn on the silk thing."

But Ax was already morphing into the wolf spider, so I hurried to catch up. By the time Ax and I were in spider morph, the others had all become cockroaches.

<Man, you two are ugly at this scale,> Rachel said. <Jeez, I don't ever need to see another spider my own size again.>

<We're ugly? You want to know what *you* look like right now? You look like dinner,> I said, laughing evilly. <Juicy cockroach. This spider morph is hungry, and you look tasty.>

<Marco, get a grip,> Jake said patiently. <Let's do this.>

<I'll demorph and step on your ugly butt,> Rachel growled.

From where I was standing in the gravel of the rooftop, the pipe looked like a round skyscraper. It extended above the roof by about a foot, which is quite a distance when you're half an inch high.

I scampered around the pipe. One side had been splashed with tar. It would be easy to grip. I raced easily up the pipe to stand precariously on the lip.

I could feel a breeze blowing up from the blackness beneath me. It was like standing on the edge of the Grand Canyon. The pipe went down through all three stories and an extra underground story. Four floors. Bad enough when you're human size. A million miles when you're a spider.

Ax came crawling up to teeter alongside me.

<Oooookay,> I said. <Now comes the fun part.>

I tried to search the spider brain, looking for the subtle, secret signals that would start me spinning silk.

Fortunately, the spider wasn't exactly Albert Einstein. It only knew how to do about four things, one of which was spin silk.

The spider body sort of . . . well . . . pushed out a strand of gooey white filament. It stuck to the edge of the pipe.

Ax did the same.

<Well, this is certainly disgusting,> I said. <Ready, Ax?>

<Yes.>

<Then . . . Yeeeeee-HAAAAAHHH!>

I sprang from the lip of the pipe into the darkness. It was so totally Spiderman.

I fell slowly down, down, down, twisting and turning my way down the pipe. Behind me a long white string grew. It braked my fall, so that I was dropping in slow motion. The spider eyes were not bad at seeing in the relative dark. A bit of moonlight followed us down part of the way as we dropped.

And then it started being fun. I kicked away from the side of the pipe and cartwheeled through the air. My web looped around Ax's, and soon we were weaving a weird silk rope.

It was cool in a way . . . till I felt a certain emptiness.

<Ax! I'm running out of web.>

<Yes, me, too.>

<How far do you think we've dropped?>

<I don't know.>

<You know which way is northwest but you don't know how far we've dropped? We could still have two stories to go,> I said.

<I think our plan has a minor flaw,> Ax said with his usual understatement. <But we are very light, small creatures. We should survive a fall. So should the others in cockroach morph.>

<Maybe. See, the problem is, there's only one way to find out if we'll survive. By dropping.>

Ax didn't say anything.

<Oh, man,> I groaned. I cut the strand of web.

And I fell. Down through the darkness, toward a landing I could only hope wouldn't kill me.

CHAPTER 21

It was a long drop.

<Aaaaahhhhhhh!>

<Aaaaahhhhhhh!>

WHAP! WHAP!

We hit something hard. We bounced. We hit again.

WHAP! WHAP!

<You okay?> Jake called down.

<Oh, yeah, I'm great,> I said. <I fell about a billion feet and landed on a steel trampoline. Couldn't be better.>

<Sarcasm,> Rachel commented coolly. <He must be okay.>

<Laugh now, Rachel. We'll see how much you laugh when it's *your* turn.>

The plan was for Ax and me to create a silk cable the others in cockroach morph would be able to climb down. That way, they wouldn't all have to go spider. Not that it would have helped, anyway.

<We're coming down,> Jake said. <When we reach the end of the silk we'll jump. If you two survived, we will. Nothing kills a cockroach.>

<Why don't you stand right beneath me, Marco?> Rachel suggested. <You can break my fall.>

Ax and I scurried out of the way. A few seconds later, after they had clambered down to the end of our silk . . .

WHAP! WHAP! WHAP! Three cockroaches landed nearby.

<Where are we?> Jake asked.

<It's pretty dark. Who knows?> I answered. <It's a heating/air-conditioning vent, I guess. Erek said it would be part of the furnace system. Supposedly we go west a hundred feet or so, then drop down, then go across the furnace, then down again, then right. Then we're at the edge of the High Security Room, where the real trouble starts.>

<Excuse me? Did someone say furnace?> Cassie asked.

<Yeah. I said furnace.>

<Does it occur to any of you that the furnace might actually come on?> Cassie said.

133

<Not till right this minute,> I said.

<It's not very cold out,> Rachel pointed out.

<Okay, I've *seriously* changed my mind,> I said. <Let's go home.>

Of course, no one listened to me. We scrabbled along the steel floor, two spiders and three cockroaches. Our rough claws seemed to make a horrible din on the metal, scuffing and scratching. But it probably wouldn't have sounded like anything to a human.

As we ran, there was more and more dust on the floor of the vent. It was weird, like walking through dried leaves. My eight legs kicked through it, and it swirled behind me as I passed. Eventually the dust became as thick as a carpet, although in reality it was probably no more than a few millimeters thick.

Every ten feet or so there would be a grilled opening. Through the massive upright bars I could see offices. The light in the offices was very dim, just the glow of computer screen savers and red or green function lights. But it helped us to find our way through the darkness of the vent.

Then . . .

<What's that?> Rachel yelled. She was the farthest back. <Uh-oh. Something coming! I feel the vibrations! Something big!>

She took off. I took off. We all took off.

Now I could feel the vibrations, too. Quick, confused-sounding footsteps. And a dragging sound, like something was being hauled.

I ran. To my left, another spider. Ax. Ahead of me, two roaches, almost as big as I was. Rachel was just back to my right.

I couldn't exactly turn and glance over my shoulder. I had no shoulder. And I had no actual head to turn. So I paused, spun around, and in the dim light from a vent, I saw it.

Huge. Twenty times my size! A vast, horrible menace.

<A rat!> I yelled. <It's a RAT!>

The thing I'd heard dragging was its naked tail and furred abdomen. It was hungry, and it was after us.

And, unfortunately, it was faster than me.

<Go! Go! Go! It's gaining!> I yelled.

We blew at top spider and cockroach speed. Which seems really fast when you're an inch long, but isn't really that many miles per hour. A rat can do maybe five or six miles per hour. A spider is lucky to break one mph.

<We'll have to morph back!> Jake said.

<Not in here!> Cassie cried. <Not enough room.>

<Next vent,> Jake said. <We go out through the next vent.>

The next vent was about ten feet away. I couldn't turn around to look at the rat, but every hair on my spider body told me it was just inches behind me.

Yet there was something else making my hair tingle, too. Something about the breeze . . .

<YAAHHH!> I heard Jake yell.

A split second later, my spider legs were clawing air. It was like a Roadrunner cartoon. I zoomed out into space, seemed to hang there with my little feet motoring away, and then I fell.

<Oh, yes,> Ax said calmly. <Erek mentioned we had to go down again.>

WHAM! WHAM! WHAM! WHAM! WHAM!

We hit steel again, and each impact sent dust clouds swirling.

<Keep running!> Cassie cried, and fortunately, for once, I didn't argue.

Buh-BOOOOOM!

The rat dropped behind us! It was still after us! Fortunately, it was a little stunned by the impact, whereas we were outta there!

Suddenly, ahead of us, the steel floor opened up again. But instead of a drop into darkness, there was a weird, vast plain of jagged spires. Each of the spires was steel, three times as tall as my little spider body. Each metal spire opened at the top. There were hundreds of them, all arranged in perfect rows. A foul smell, something my spider mind knew nothing about, came from this field of spires.

A weird, flickering glow lit the landscape. In the eerie light, it looked like some awful grave-yard, with the spires like industrial-strength gravestones or something. I mean, it was creepy.

<What is this?> I asked.

<Let's just get going, all right?> Rachel sug-gested. <We can sightsee some other time.>

I would never have walked into that "field" if the rat hadn't been just two feet back and gain-ing again. I didn't need spider senses to know there was danger here. It screamed danger.

I stuck out one spider leg and touched the top of the nearest spire. Then another and another. I walked from spire to spire, carefully, cautiously. The cockroaches crawled and squirmed through the valleys between spires. Unable to stand nor-mally, they had to drag themselves inch by inch.

<What is this?> I asked again.

<You don't want to know,> Jake said grimly. <Let's just get out of here, okay?>

Right then it hit me. From the tone of Jake's thought-speak voice.

<Oh, man. This is the furnace, isn't it? These spires . . . the holes in the tops of them . . . it's where the gas comes out!>

<Not if no one turns on the heat,> Rachel said grimly.

Over my head now, I saw the source of the eerie glow. It was the pilot light. It was a jet of blue flame as long as my body. I could feel the heat from it, even though it seemed to be as far above my head as the ceiling of a cathedral.

The rat, smarter than we were, decided to stop at the edge of the furnace. But there was no going back. We had to cross the furnace. We had to hope the Matcom Corporation was into energy conservation and didn't waste heat. We had to pray that no one had messed with the thermostat.

Because if the heat came on . . .

HISSSSSSSSSSSSSSSSSS!

<Gas!>

The gas blew with hurricane force up through the tops of the spires. In seconds the gas would rise to the pilot light. In seconds the entire landscape would erupt in flame!

I thought I'd been moving as fast as I could move.

I was wrong. I had a whole extra speed.

Ahead of me I saw Jake, Rachel, and Ax all reach safety. Only Cassie and I were still deadly inches away from safety.

<RUN! RUN! RUNRUNRUNRUN!>

HISSSSSSSSSSSSSSSSSS!

Then . . . WHOOOOOOSH!

Fuh-WWWUUUUMMMP!

The whole world seemed to explode around me. A wall of flame . . . a hurricane of hot air. I was blown head over heels, somersaulting through air as hot as an oven.

CHAPTER 22

I somersaulted backward, hit steel floor again, and screeched like a skidding car. I plowed straight into Jake, and a split second later, Cassie plowed straight into me.

<Cassie! Cassie! Are you okay?> Jake asked.

<Yes, yes. I think so. Who can tell with this roach body?>

<I'm okay, too,> I said. <You know, just in case anyone cares.>

<I guess they like to keep this building nice and warm, eh?> Rachel said.

<That was very close to being a disaster,> Ax said. <We should thank the rat. If he had not chased us, we would have been crossing those gas jets several seconds later.>

That was not a nice picture to think of. We would have fried, sizzled, and popped open faster than we could even try to think about de-morphing.

<That would have left a big wad of Marco mass floating in Z-space,> I muttered. I could joke about it, but I was quivering inside.

The rest of the trip through the heating and air-conditioning system was calm. But that just gave me time to think about the close call. One second slower, and I'd have gone out as a roasted spider.

<There are walls up here,> Jake warned from the head of our little pack of singed bugs. <No, wait, not walls. Like a maze. Like Erek said.>

We traveled through a series of switchbacks, around a steel panel, then back around another. It was a light-blocking system. It would block out every last photon of light that might come through the vent.

Then we came to the edge of a drop. Beyond it, I knew, was the High Security Room itself — the location of the Pemalite crystal.

We were six feet up. We had to drop, and then stay within two feet of the wall. Any movement farther toward the center of the huge room, and we would set off pressure sensors in the floor.

By this time, we were used to falling.

<Next I want to try jumping out of a plane.

141

Without a parachute,> I said as I stepped into the black void.

It is an eerie experience falling in total darkness. You have no idea where the floor is. It's almost like you're not falling at all. Until you hit the bottom, that is.

<Stay close to the wall,> Jake reminded everyone. <Hug the wall and demorph.>

I was relieved to be human again. But my human eyes were no better than spider eyes at penetrating the darkness. It was darker than any night. Darker than hiding in a closet at midnight. This was the darkness of being buried alive.

"There could be six Hork-Bajir standing three inches away, and we wouldn't know it," I said, in a whisper that seemed to be deadened by the darkness itself.

"That's a nice thought," Rachel said dryly.

<Even a single photon of light would set off the light sensors,> Ax said. <This is complete darkness.>

"And according to Erek, if we stepped two feet away from the wall, we'd run into a maze of ultrasensitive wires. Any contact and the alarm goes off. We have to travel forty feet without touching a wire. Without touching the floor or ceiling or walls," Jake reminded us.

"Let's morph. We'll be able to see then,"

Cassie said. "Or maybe not *see*, exactly, but you know what I mean."

What she meant was that we would be able to echolocate. Kinda like the dolphin morph. We would be able to make very fast, ultrahigh sounds that the human ear would not even hear.

Those sounds would vibrate off any solid object and send back a sort of sound picture.

At least, that's what we hoped. We had been planning to practice and find out if it was true. Instead, we were morphing without any knowledge of what we were getting into.

"Someday we'll think all this is funny," I said. "You know, if we happen to live long enough."

I focused my mind on the bat morph we had each acquired. They aren't as creepy as people think. Certainly not as creepy as morphing a spider. This particular bat was very small, just a few inches long. It looked like a mouse, with huge ears and the face of a Pekinese dog. If you forgot about the leathery wings, it was just another basic mammal.

But this was one case where the weirdness wasn't something you saw. I couldn't see anything. Nothing. I couldn't see myself shrinking, the ground rushing up at me. I couldn't see the way my legs shrank to almost nothing and brown fur sprouted from my body. I couldn't see the way my fingers grew so long and a paper-thin leather web filled the spaces between them.

I saw none of it. I didn't even know I was a bat, until my bat brain sent an order for me to open my mouth and chirp out a pulse of sound.

I fired a string of superfast sound pulses. Like making a loud machine-gun sound, only a lot higher, and way, way faster.

And then . . .

<Whoa, ho!> I said.

The entire black, pitch-black, invisible room, had just lit up.

It wasn't like seeing, exactly. It was like . . . like feeling, almost. Except it was like you were feeling from a distance. I *felt* a vast room. I *felt* thousands of wires strung taut, up and down, left to right, at angles.

And, at the center of the room, beyond the maze of wires, I *felt* a raised, flat surface, and a sort of pedestal. There were curling wires coming from the top of the pedestal.

All that came in a flash. Then it was gone. The others each fired off their own echolocating blasts, but I couldn't *feel* their sounds as clearly.

<Okay, *that* is cool,> Rachel said. <That is way cool.>

<The wires seem awfully close together,> Cassie worried. <I wish we'd had time to try out

these wings. I guess all we can do is hope for the best. Trust the bat to do the flying.>

<Abandon yourself to the Force, Cassie Skywalker,> I said.

<Thanks, Darth. You first.>

<*Me* first? Oh.> Suddenly, I didn't feel at all like laughing. I licked my lips with my little bat tongue. Assuming I had lips. I wasn't sure.

I opened my wings. I spread them wide and thought, *Well, this should be interesting.* I tested the wings cautiously. They moved differently than bird wings. More like I was reaching out with each stroke to grab the air and push it behind me.

<Okay. Here goes.>

I fired an echolocating burst and took off.

Fired again! There were tight strings all around me!

Left!

Left again!

Down!

No, up!

Right, left, right, right, straight up!

Again and again the high-pitched sound machine gun fired. Again and again I dodged, millimeters from a wire.

It was insane! It was so fast my human brain was three steps behind. It was instantaneous. It was impossible! The speed, the agility, the instant translation of the echolocating blasts.

And suddenly, I was through! I was through the wires.

I landed on the table in the center of the room. It was all over in ten seconds of lunatic flight.

<Okay, now *that* is a roller-coaster ride! Yes!> I said, incredibly jazzed from having made it. <Yes!>

The others came, one by one. I could watch them fly, seeing them in my echolocating flashes.

Everyone made it. And we were feeling pretty good about it, too. It was a rush.

<We did it!> I said.

<These bats can fly!> Rachel added.

<Is that the crystal?> Cassie asked.

Ax fired a burst and said, <That must be it.>

It was no bigger than a grape. It rested on a small pedestal. Wires — not the sensor wires, but curling electrical-type wires, edged in all around it. But the crystal itself was not attached to anything. It just lay there, where anyone could grab it.

It made a low sort of humming noise. I know it makes no sense, but it was almost like that crystal was alive.

<Um . . . I have a stupid question,> I said. <How do we grab this thing?>

For about ten seconds, no one said a word.

<We don't have hands,> Cassie said, pointing out the obvious.

<We can grab it in our mouths,> Rachel said. <Right? Bats eat moths and stuff. They must have pretty strong jaws. Strong enough to get that crystal back to the air vent.>

<Oh, duh. Of course,> Jake said, sounding relieved. <I'll do it.>

<I believe that may not work,> Ax said.

<Jake?> Cassie said. <Jake? If you have a crystal in your mouth, how do you fire the echolocating burst?>

At which point we were suddenly no longer feeling so good.

<I believe our plan now has somewhat of a flaw,> Ax said quietly.

CHAPTER 23

<S>ee? We should never get cocky,> Cassie said. <It's tempting the irony gods.>

<Irony gods?> Ax asked.

<Yeah,> Cassie said. <The bitter spirits who wait around till you get cocky, then hammer you.>

<These are *real*?>

<No, of course not,> Cassie said impatiently. <How do we get out of here with that crystal?>

<We power our way out,> Rachel said.

Ax said, <Erek's opinion was that there were many guards here in this building.>

<We didn't see any on our way through the shafts,> Jake remarked. <But Erek's been pretty

accurate so far. I have a feeling if he says there are guards here, there are *guards* here.>

<No choice,> Rachel said. <We morph whatever we have that's big, mean, and nasty, then slam our way out of this place.>

<Speaking of irony gods,> I muttered.

<What do you mean?> Rachel asked.

<I mean, we came here to get this Pemalite crystal so the Chee could be free to be violent. And now, despite all our clever planning, all our sneakiness and subtlety, we're stuck in the end going for total Schwarzenegger.>

<Rachel's right,> Jake said. He sighed. <We're looking at a fighting retreat.>

Cassie said, <I think there's a door over there. Try echolocating. You'll see a raised rectangular outline. I think it's a door.>

<Yep,> Jake agreed. <Morph out, keep that direction in mind. Remorph, and be ready to haul butt for that door. Head for any way out of this building. Don't stand and fight, just try to force your way past anyone who comes after us.>

It was times like this I was glad Jake was our so-called leader. We all knew what we had to do, but someone had to actually *say* it. And boy, was I glad it wasn't me.

<I have such a bad feeling about this,> I muttered.

149

Have you ever watched those old war movies where the Americans would be heading for some enemy beach? You know, they'd be in a little boat, riding through the surf, getting ready to jump out on a beach that was going to be chewed up by machine-gun bullets and mortars?

That's what this felt like. Like we were pretty calm now, but in a few seconds it was going to be life and death. Things would happen very fast. And none of it was going to be good.

I morphed back to human. Then I focused my mind on the morph I liked for fighting.

It was still absolutely dark, so I didn't see my body grow big and hairy. But I could feel my shoulders bulk up beyond anything any body-builder ever even dreamed of. I could feel the strength. Strength like no human could ever possess. It was comforting to think that I was stronger than three, four, maybe five strong men. But not even the gorilla is invincible.

<Everyone ready?> Jake asked.

There in the darkness, near enough to touch, but invisible, was enough power to shred a small army. Jake was in his tiger morph. Cassie had gone wolf. Rachel was one of the few animals mightier than my gorilla: She was a full-grown, massively powerful grizzly bear. And Ax . . . well, Ax was Ax. And trust me, when you've seen an

Andalite in battle, you know that tail is all he needs.

<Ready? Why, I'm looking forward to it,> I said, trying to sound like I wasn't scared silly.

<I'll go first,> Rachel said. And before anyone had time to object . . .

HHHRRRRRAAAAWWWWRRR!

Rachel barreled past me, hitting me and practically spinning me around like a top.

A microsecond later . . .

ScreeEEEEET! ScreeEEEEET! ScreeEEEEET! The alarm was deafening.

The others barreled after her. I hesitated for just a moment while I felt in the dark for the Pemalite crystal. Aside from Ax, I was the only one with hands.

Then I went after them. I plunged wildly into total darkness with a tiny crystal in my massive fist.

Rachel tore a path through the alarm wires, and I could feel where she had gone. I slammed into Ax, then bounced into Jake, then suddenly — WHAM! — hit the wall.

ScreeEEEEET! ScreeEEEET! ScreeEEEET!

Ka-RRRRUNCH! A loud, screeching, tearing noise.

Sudden light! I could see.

Man, it was a relief to be able to see something at least.

Dim light came through the door. Or what was left of the door, after Rachel had given the door a thousand pounds or so of mad, ready-to-fight grizzly. The door was splinters. It was steel, and it was *still* splinters.

I saw a flash of orange and black, moving fast but almost delicately — Jake, in tiger morph. Cassie the wolf followed him. Right behind her was the one animal that wasn't from anywhere on Earth.

There was a hallway outside. Jake said <Left!> and we went left.

Past doorways, past offices, past normal things like copiers and computers and fax machines and desks and cubicles, we ran. Rachel was in the lead, a huge, lumbering truck on four legs. Her roars mixed with the endless scream of the alarms.

ScreeEEEEET! ScreeEEEEET! ScreeEEEEET!

Suddenly, another door, a dead end. Rachel hit it with her shoulder, and the door was gone. There was a big room beyond. High ceilings, open space, a lobby sort of room. Windows! I could see faint stars through the tinted glass.

Escape was just a hundred feet away.

Freedom! Life!

And all that stood in our way was twenty men: human-Controllers, armed with automatic rifles.

And behind them, two dozen or more Hork-Bajir warriors.

Rachel's bear had very poor vision, especially in this dim light. <Hork-Bajir?> she asked.

<Yep,> I said.

<How many?>

<Too many. Way too many.>

CHAPTER 24

ScreeEEEET! ScreeEEEEET! ScreeEEEET!

The alarm was howling. And then, a far worse sound:

Cha-KLICK!

The human-Controllers had cocked their rifles, chambering a round. If they fired, we'd be blown apart before we could twitch.

A human-Controller stepped out in front. She was a nice-looking, middle-aged woman wearing normal street clothes. She had bleached blond hair. She could have been someone's grandmother.

"So. The Andalite bandits," she said. Her face was twitching with tension, but she tried to sound calm. "You've done me a big favor. When I turn you over to Visser Three he'll promote me two grades. Maybe three!"

<Or he may decide to destroy you for letting us get this far,> Ax said coolly.

"Surrender. You can't escape," the woman snapped. "I'd rather take you alive, but the Visser would still be happy to have your corpses."

We stared at her. And we stared at the muzzles of the twenty automatic rifles that were leveled at us.

I held up my hand. Between my thick, brute fingers I held the Pemalite crystal.

The woman turned as pale as her hair. "Give me that."

I shook my big gorilla head.

"Lower those guns," the woman snapped.

"What?" some guy behind her yelled. "We have them! We have them cold!"

The woman's jaw twitched again, but she stayed in control. "What do you think a bullet would do to that crystal?"

"But the odds that a bullet would hit the crystal . . . It's not going to happen."

The woman smiled grimly. "That crystal is worth more than the mother ship and everything in it," she said. Then she started yelling. "You want to shoot? Go ahead, fool! If you hit the crystal, you can explain it to Visser Three."

She got a grip on herself while the guy who

had spoken out decided he was not interested in explaining anything to Visser Three.

"All human-Controllers, back. Weapons on safety," the woman snapped.

The rifles faltered, then lowered toward the ground. But I knew better than to breathe a sigh of relief. See, I knew what was coming next.

The woman looked right at me and smiled. "Hork-Bajir, forward."

The Andalite who'd given us our powers had told us that the Hork-Bajir had once been a gentle, decent race before they were all enslaved by the Yeerks. All Hork-Bajir were Controllers now.

But it was hard to believe the Hork-Bajir had ever been the sweethearts of the galaxy. They were death on two legs: seven feet tall, eight, if you counted the forward-raked blades that protruded from the top of their snake-heads. They had blades at their elbows, blades at their wrists, blades at their knees. They had huge claw-feet like tyrannosaurs, and a short, thick tail that ended in cruel-looking spikes.

They were walking razor blades. All sharp edges and lightning speed.

I've fought Hork-Bajir before. And I can count. Two dozen Hork-Bajir was at least a dozen more than we had any hope of defeating.

Then, behind the Hork-Bajir, beyond the retreating human-Controllers, outside the building, staring horror-stricken through the glass, I saw Erek.

Erek, who could do nothing at all to help us. Who was helpless to do anything but witness our slaughter. I felt like throwing up. The fear was all over me. The fear was surging through me, washing over me, drowning me from inside and out.

We were going to lose.

We were going to die.

And life, any kind of life almost, is so much better than being dead.

"Attack," the woman said. Her voice was nearly a whisper.

The Hork-Bajir leaped forward, a wall of slashing, whirling blades.

Right in front of me!

SEEEEWWW!

A huge Hork-Bajir slashed and a bright red line cut across my black leather chest!

I swung my fist and hit the Hork-Bajir hard enough to fold him in two. But another leaped over him and came at me. I blocked his arm, but he kicked at me with his clawed foot.

I fell back. I looked down and saw a hole in my stomach.

A hole! I could see the gorilla's insides! My insides. My insides!

<Ahhhhh!> I screamed in thought-speak, as the gorilla bellowed in agony.

157

The Hork-Bajir leaped on top of me. I swung again and knocked his legs out from under him. He toppled down, but landed beside me. My left hand went to his throat and I squeezed. I squeezed with all the strength I had. The Hork-Bajir slashed at me again and opened a gash in my hairy arm. But I kept my grip tight.

I screamed as the Hork-Bajir twitched and scrabbled wildly and began to jerk uncontrollably.

The battle raged all around me.

Screams. Cries. Bellows of animal rage. The garbled roars of the Hork-Bajir. Even the guttural roar of the human-Controllers, who watched and cheered the Hork-Bajir on.

I saw Jake leap through the air and close his jaws around a Hork-Bajir's face.

I saw Rachel swing her paw and open up a Hork-Bajir like someone cleaning a fish.

I saw Cassie dodging swiftly, biting, backing away, lunging to bite again, red foam flying from her muzzle.

And Ax, striking again . . . again . . . again with the deadly speed and perfect accuracy of his Andalite tail.

But we were losing. It would be over in a few seconds. We were losing.

<Oh, God!> someone screamed. Maybe it was me, I don't know.

<Help! Help! Get him off me!>
<Look out!>
<No! Nooooo!>

It was all one combined thought-speech scream.

And still the alarm howled its screeEEEEET!

I felt my grip weaken on the throat of the Hork-Bajir. But it didn't matter anymore. It was safe to let him go.

My vision was red. Red and fading.

I felt a sharp stab as another Hork-Bajir sunk a blade into my gorilla heart.

None of it mattered, though. It was all coming to an end . . . all coming to an end. . . .

Through a red mist I saw a face on the other side of the glass. Erek. Somehow, in the battle, I had ended up not far from the wall of windows.

Erek was just a few feet away. Just on the other side of the glass.

I felt something hard in my palm. The crystal.

I crawled. A vicious Hork-Bajir kick, and I went sprawling right against the glass.

<Oh . . . no,> I said. I could see the damage the kick had done. I was dead. I could feel my brain shutting down.

Human-Controllers were closing in around me, hammering me with the butts of their rifles.

With my last ounce of strength, I rammed my fist through the glass.

159

I felt strong fingers pry open my hand. I felt the fingers lift out the crystal.

And then . . . later, much later, someone slapped my face.

"Morph back, Marco. Morph back! Do it!"

CHAPTER 25

I woke up on the ground. Not a floor, the ground. Dirt and leaves.

I sat up very fast. I looked at my body.

"Human!" I said. I wanted to cry from the sheer relief of being myself again. Myself and alive.

I looked around. Jake. Cassie. Rachel. Ax. All there! All human! Except for Ax, of course.

Tobias was perched in the tree above us.

Someone else was there, too. I heard a voice sobbing.

"You okay, Marco?" Jake asked.

"Yeah. Yeah. Oh, man. Man, I was so close to being dead!"

"You were," Jake said solemnly. "He gave you an electric shock to start your heart again."

"Who did?"

Jake jerked his head toward the source of the crying. It was Erek, sitting in the dirt with his head down.

"Where are we?" I asked.

"Little bunch of trees, just down from Matcom. Or what's left of Matcom."

"How did we get here? How did we get out of that place? We were toast!"

Cassie came over and sat beside me. "You saved us by getting the crystal to Erek. He used it. He rewrote his programming. He's the one who . . ." She looked away. "He . . ."

"He took care of the Hork-Bajir," Rachel said. "I saw some of it. I was still conscious."

I was confused. "How did Erek take care of the Hork-Bajir?"

<He destroyed them all,> Ax said.

I almost laughed. "Erek took out two dozen Hork-Bajir?"

No one laughed with me. Erek had stopped sobbing. I thought, *Why would a robot cry?*

<All the Hork-Bajir,> Ax said. <All the human-Controllers. All of them.>

I stood up. I could see the Matcom building. It was only a few hundred yards away. There was a big hole in the front glass. I had a very bad feeling about what was on the other side of that glass.

All I could think of to say was, "*All* of them?"

"It lasted about ten seconds," Rachel said. She closed her eyes, trying not to remember what she had seen. But I guess the images weren't easily shut out. She opened her eyes again, and to my utter amazement, I saw tears.

That's what brought the horror home to me — Rachel's tears.

<It was extremely brutal,> Ax said. <Very brutal, and very swift. He carried us here. He revived you. He even reattached my arm.>

I saw a scar on Ax's left arm.

"He hasn't said anything since then," Cassie said sadly. "He won't talk to any of us."

"He saved us, though, right?" I said.

"Yeah," Cassie agreed, smiling a deeply sad smile. "He saved our lives. And lost his own soul."

I went to Erek. I wanted to thank him. I wanted to tell him he'd done what was right. He'd beaten the bad guys. Saved the good guys.

He stood up as I came over.

"You okay, man?" I asked him.

He looked at me with holographic human eyes. Maybe he had to *choose* to make them cry. Maybe he had to *choose* to give them that empty, hollow look. I don't know what the connection is

163

between the android Chee and his projected human body. But his expression answered my question.

No. Erek was not okay.

"You saved our lives, Erek," I said.

"How do you . . . how do you live with the memory?" he asked me.

I knew what he meant. See, win or lose, right or wrong, the memory of violence sits inside your head. It sits there, like some lump you can't quite swallow. It sits there, a black hole that darkens hope, and eats away at everyday happiness like a cancer. It's the shadow you take into your own heart and try to live with.

I shrugged. "I guess I try not to think about it. I try and forget. And after a while, the nightmares don't happen as much."

Erek put a finger to his head. "Android," he said. He made a bitter, ruined smile. "I can't forget. See? I can never forget . . . anything."

I looked at him. Already in my own human mind, the memories of that night's horror were fading. The flash of blades and the pain and the sickening feeling of my fist closing around the Hork-Bajir's throat . . . they were being covered over by scar tissue.

What if I could never forget?

What if all those memories were fresh forever?

I realized then why the Pemalites had forbidden their creatures to kill. The Chee lived forever. Forever was a long time to remember what Erek had done.

"I'm sorry," I said.

Erek nodded. "Yes." He held out his clenched fist, palm down. I knew what he was doing. I didn't want it. But I held out my own hand, and took the Pemalite crystal from him.

"I've changed my programming back," Erek said. "We . . . I . . . maybe at times I can tell you things. Information. But I'll never fight again. I can't join this war, my friend."

He walked away. We went to our homes and crawled into beds our parents never knew we'd left.

I was beyond exhausted. But I couldn't sleep. Too many images. Too many memories. And I was afraid of the nightmares.

There are evil things in life, and I guess there are times when a human being has to fight those evils.

I closed my eyes and wandered lost and afraid through my nightmares.

And already, my mind was forgetting.

CHAPTER 26

"Yeah! Yeah! Go boy!"

Homer ran flat out, kicking up divots of sand as the Frisbee soared over his head. With a burst of speed, Homer got out in front of the Frisbee, jumped, pivoted in midair, and snatched the disc out of the air. His jump carried him to the water's edge and he landed in the surf.

"Yeah! Good boy!" Jake said.

"Not bad," I said. "He's not quite that Frisbee dog we saw on TV, but he's not bad."

"Hey, that was a *professional* Frisbee dog. Homer's just in it for the sport. Homer doesn't even have any endorsements."

Homer came trotting back across the sand with the Frisbee in his mouth.

166

It was a week after our battle for the Pemalite crystal. Jake and I were at the beach. Tobias was high overhead, riding the thermals. I didn't know where the others were.

And my hair had finally grown out a little. But I'd gotten used to having it shorter. I decided to keep it that way, just to spite everyone.

There weren't that many people on the beach because it was a little too chilly for lying out. Instead, people came down and flew kites, or walked along, looking for sand dollars and shells. And they played with their dogs.

Jake knelt down and tried to take the Frisbee from Homer. But Homer, like just about every dog in all of history, refused to give it up.

"They just don't get the point of this whole game," I said. "You throw, they catch, they bring it back for you to throw again. Why is that so hard to figure out?"

Jake scratched right behind Homer's ear, and Homer dropped the Frisbee. "Oh, they know how to play the game, all right," Jake said with a laugh. "For them, the game is 'I throw, they catch, they bring it back, they get a good head scratch, *then* they give up the Frisbee.'"

But just then, Homer lost all interest in the Frisbee. Two dogs were trotting by, tails in the air. Homer jogged over to greet them. They sniffed each other by way of introduction, then took off,

167

running like the giddy, happy, always-excited, dog goofs they were.

It made me smile to watch them.

"It must have been a nice place," I said.

Jake knew exactly what I was talking about. "Yeah. A planet where the people were as sweet and decent as dogs. Yeah, that would have been okay."

"I ran into Erek at the 7-Eleven yesterday," I said. "I think he was looking for a place to 'accidentally' run into me. Anyway, he gave me a phone number. He says it's an absolutely safe phone. He says the Yeerks couldn't tap it or trace it if they tried."

"Yeah? So?" Jake asked.

I shrugged. "So, he says if we ever need him we could leave a message at that number. And if he has something to tell us, he'll record a message for us."

"Huh," Jake grunted. "Think anything will ever come of it?"

"I don't know," I said honestly. "But I think the Chee are going to go on fighting the Yeerks. They'll just be doing it in their own way."

I reached into my pocket and drew out the small, diamondlike crystal. "I still have this, by the way. I don't know what to do about it. Erek didn't even want to talk about it. But this is the most powerful computer ever created. It could rewrite the Chees' programming. It could take over every computer on Earth. The Pemalite crystal. We almost died getting it. What am I supposed to do with it?"

Jake and I stood there, looking down at more power than any human had ever held in his hand.

Suddenly, I realized we weren't alone.

Homer and the other two dogs were standing right in front of us, watching us. I know this sounds crazy, but I swear some flicker of intelligence appeared in those laughing dog eyes.

The three of them looked at us, and we looked back.

I held out my hand, palm up, to show the dogs the crystal. Homer scarfed the crystal out of my hand as if it were a dog biscuit. But he didn't swallow it, just held it in his teeth, where it glittered like a diamond.

The three dogs turned and ran down the beach. They ran into the surf and splashed out into the water, paddling for a dozen feet or so.

Then they came back to shore, and had a glorious time shaking themselves violently and spraying water all over two old ladies who were hunting shells.

Maybe someday the Pemalite crystal will wash back up on some beach somewhere. Maybe by the time it does, we'll be as wise as the race that created it.

"Homer!" Jake yelled. He threw the Frisbee.

And all three of the dogs, happy, silly, loving fools that they were, went racing after it.

8:42 P.M.

It was crowded inside the Bug fighter. Especially because Ax takes up a lot of room.

But we huddled together and looked over Ax's shoulders as he worked the controls. And we looked past Ax, out through the transparent panels at the front of the Bug fighter.

<This ship is very difficult to handle,> Ax said. <The design is strange. Some controls are psychotronic. But others require physical handling. Unfortunately, those controls are designed for Taxxons. They have more hands than I.>

"Can we do anything to help?" I asked.

<Someone should take the weapons station,> Ax said.

"Cool," Marco said. He leaped forward, but I was closer.

I slipped into the area beside Ax. Ax's pilot

"seat" wasn't a seat at all, of course. Taxxons are like huge centipedes, so they can't really sit. Which was good, because Ax doesn't sit, either.

But the weapons station was built for Hork-Bajir. Hork-Bajir are seven feet tall and have thick, spikey tails, but they do sit.

"No *way* you should handle the weapons," Marco said, leaning over my shoulder. "I kick your butt in video games."

"Yeah, right," I said. "In some alternate universe, maybe."

"Grab the joystick," Marco suggested.

As strange as it seems, there actually was a joystick. It was for much bigger hands than mine, and the two buttons on it were clumsy to reach. But it was a joystick.

"Maybe I should test the weapons," I said to Ax.

<Yes,> he said tersely, distracted.

We were rising up through the atmosphere. We were above the clouds already. I could see brief flashes of the lights of the city down below, but mostly it was clouds and more clouds.

But we weren't rising as fast as I would have expected. Ax was definitely working to control the ship.

I looked ahead, saw nothing in the way, and pressed one of the buttons on the joystick. Nothing.

Ax glanced over. <That was the safety. The Dracon beam should be armed now. See the screen before you? The red circle is how you aim. Use a combination of moving the joystick, but also use your mind.>

Marco put his hand on my shoulder. "Phasers on full power!" he said in a Captain Picard English accent. "Arm photon torpedoes! If the Borg want a fight, we'll give them one! Make it so!"

I moved the joystick and watched the target circle track across the screen. It still showed nothing but starry sky. That should be safe enough.

I squeezed the second button.

TSEWWWW! TSEWWWW!

Twin red beams of light fired forward, converging too far away for me to see.

"Yes! Most splendid!" Marco yelled.

"Okay, that *was* cool," I admitted, trying not to cackle like an idiot with his first video game.

"Boys with their toys," Cassie teased gently.

<Prince Jake?> Ax said. <I must apologize.>

"Why?"

<I did not at first realize: This Bug fighter's cloaking field is not working.>

It took a few seconds for me to track on that. "You mean . . . people can see us?"

<The clouds will hide us from people on the ground,> Ax said. <But human radar will observe us. In fact, they have already observed us.>

"Uh-oh. Maybe we better get higher," I suggested.

<Yes. But we are rising slowly. I don't know why. And there are two objects approaching us.>

"Probably just airliners," Rachel said.

<The objects are moving at one-and-a-half times the speed of sound,> Ax said.

"Okay, that's not a passenger plane," Marco said.

I groaned. "Military jets. Oh, man, it's the Air Force after us. They're 'good guys.' They're on our side. We can't shoot them down."

Suddenly . . .

SWOOOOOSH!

SWOOOOOSH!

Two pale gray jets blew past us. The backwash rattled the Bug fighter.

<I can access their radio signals,> Ax said. And a second later we heard the voice of one of the pilots.

"Um . . . Base Control, I . . . um . . . Bogie is of an unknown type. Say again, unknown type."

"Definitely unknown," the other pilot said. "Way unknown."

"We're coming around for another pass."

I looked at Ax. "We really don't want to get shot down by a couple of F-sixteens."

<No, Prince Jake. That would be embarrassing. I believe I now know how to increase —>

FAH-WHOOOOOOOM!

Suddenly, we were outta there. Out of the clouds. Out of the atmosphere.

"Yes! This thing can move!" Marco exulted. "We need to buy this game."

We heard a fainter, crackling voice over the radio. "Did you see that? Did you see that thing move, Colonel? Did you see that? What the —"

Then we were out of range, still zooming straight up into black space. Below us I could see the curvature of the earth. It looked just like one of those pictures the shuttle astronauts take from up in orbit.

"That's so beautiful," Cassie said. "Look at that! You can see daylight coming up over the Red Sea."

<Excuse me,> Tobias said, <but I don't think the Red Sea is exactly on the way to Washington, D.C.>

"Yeah, I guess not," I said. Although it was such a wonderful sight that I almost didn't want to worry about where we were going. "Ax, maybe we'd better slow down, get some idea of where Washington is and —"

<No! No!> Ax snapped.

I was shocked. Ax is always polite.

<No, Prince Jake,> he said, a little more calmly. <We cannot slow down.>

"What's the matter?" Cassie asked him.

Ax pointed at one of the view screens before him. On the screen I saw stars. Then the moon came into view, a vast gray-and-white lightbulb.

And silhouetted against the glowing moon was a shape. It was like some medieval battle-ax. The rear half was a two-headed blade. From the middle, like an ax handle, extended a long shaft. At the end of the shaft was a triangular head, very much like an arrow's point.

It was black on black. And even if you had never seen it before and had no idea what it was, you'd know right away it was death.

I *had* seen it. I *knew* what it was.

"The Blade ship," I whispered.

The Blade ship of Visser Three.

Alone in a jungle. Lost in time. Facing certain death.
That is, if Visser Three doesn't get them first.

ANIMORPHS

<I suspect we have moved backward in time. There are now two of each of us. One here, one there. At the same time.>

"That's good," Marco said.

<No,> Ax said solemnly. <It's not good. The two groups will annihilate each other. We'd cease to exist.>

If Ax was right, the *Sario Rip* would end, and the universe would have two Jakes and two Cassies, and would eliminate them both.

We had two hours left.

ANIMORPHS #11: THE FORGOTTEN

COMING IN SEPTEMBER

K.A. Applegate

JOIN US

ANIMORPHS™

K. A. APPLEGATE

Order your books. . .before it's too late!